"I came to help you, not hold you back," Tarrys said.

Charlie settled his hand on her jaw and rubbed his thumb over her cheek. "I was being an ass. I thought if I pushed you hard enough, you'd beg off and tell me you had someplace else to go."

"I don't."

"I know." He took her hands and rubbed his thumbs over her soft skin, the friction going through him like electricity. His gut reaction was to pull her closer, but he felt a tension in her. A resistance. So he held her hands and met her gaze. *Fell* into her gaze. Why had he never noticed that her eyes were deep as the ocean, bottomless wells of violet? Why did she have this pull on him?

Dear Reader,

Here, at last, is the long-awaited third book in the Esri series that began with *The Dark Gate* and continued with *Dark Deceiver*. While you needn't have read either of the previous books to enjoy this one, I hope you'll be intrigued enough by the story and the world to eventually pick them up. The climactic ending of the four-book Esri series, *Warrior Rising*, will be available soon from Mills & Boon Nocturne.

For more information about all of my books, and to learn more about the world of the Esri, please visit my website, www.pamelapalmer.net.

Happy reading!

Pamela Palmer

A Warrior's Desire

PAMELA PALMER

First published in Great Britain 2012
by Mills & Boon,
an imprint of Harlequin (UK) Limited,
Large Print edition 2012
Harlequin (UK) Limited, Eton House,
18-24 Paradise Road, Richmond, Surrey TW9 1SR

© Pamela Palmer Poulsen 2012

ISBN: 978 0 263 23038 3

Harlequin (UK) policy is to use papers that are
natural, renewable and recyclable products and made
from wood grown in sustainable forests. The logging
and manufacturing process conform to the legal
environmental regulations of the country of origin.

Printed and bound in Great Britain
by CPI Antony Rowe, Chippenham, Wiltshire

Pamela Palmer is a *New York Times* and *USA TODAY* bestselling author. When her initial career goal of captaining starships didn't pan out, Pamela turned to engineering, satisfying her desire for adventure with books and daydreams until finally succumbing to the need to create worlds of her own. She lives and writes in the suburbs of Washington, DC.

Many, many thanks to the wonderful team at my publisher, especially my editor, Ann Leslie Tuttle. And special thanks to Laurin Wittig and Anne Shaw Moran who read and edit everything I write. I'd be lost without you. Thanks to Tommy Gardner for the intriguing discussion of what a Navy SEAL might take on a mission into Esria. And as always, thanks to my family and my real life hero, Keith, who supports me in a thousand ways and does all the grocery shopping. Now *that's* a hero.

Chapter 1

I *can't go back there.*

Slavery. Pain. Degradation. Her body controlled by another's mind, every action orchestrated by her master's intent, her free will ripped away. Eliminated. Destroyed.

I will not go back to that.

With shaking hands, Tarrys dumped the leftover coffee into the kitchen sink as the two brothers, Charlie and Harrison Rand, argued behind her in the living room of the small apartment she shared with Aunt Myrtle in downtown Washington, D.C. Their every word scraped at her conscience.

"Dammit, Charlie, you'll never get through Esria alive. It's suicide."

Charlie Rand made a sharp sound of disgust. "It's not suicide. Give me a little more credit than that, Harrison. But even if it is, what choice do we have? If we don't stop the Esri, we're as good as dead anyway."

It was almost three in the morning, but the meeting of the Sitheen Resistance—the mere handful of humans who knew of the Esri invasion and could actually fight it—had just ended. The others had left or retired to bed, the plan set.

When the gate into Esria opened at midnight tonight, Charlie Rand was going through.

And would almost certainly die.

I could help him.

Tarrys's stomach clenched painfully. Shaking her head against the whispers of her conscience, she soaped the sponge and began cleaning the coffee carafe. She'd prayed it wouldn't come to this. Prayed the humans would find a way to seal the gate between the worlds, shutting the Esri out once and for all, leaving her on this side.

Safe. *Free.*

Because, though they treated her as one of them—as a human—she wasn't.

She looked human though, at five feet tall, a small one. Her body might be slender, but for the first time in her life she had food aplenty and had started to develop true curves. Even her hair had begun to grow and now covered her scalp in a sleek, dark cap of which she was immensely pleased.

Yes, she might pass for human easily enough, but she wasn't mortal. She was Marceil, one of the slave race of Esria.

Aftcr knowing frccdom and kindness, how would her heart ever survive slavery again?

"There has to be another way to seal those gates," Harrison said. "We'll find it."

"And how many more people will die in the meantime?" Charlie's angry frustration set the air to vibrating, quickening her pulse.

Tarrys grabbed the dish towel and turned to

lean against the counter as she dried the carafe, her gaze drawn to Charlie. While Harrison maintained an air of deadly calm, Charlie was living motion and muscle, passion and anger. Like his brother, he towered over her in height, his hair close-cropped and sun-streaked. But it was Charlie, with his mercurial temperament and his charmer's smile, whose presence dominated the room, heating her flesh and stealing her air.

It was Charlie Rand who made her wish she were human, a beautiful human he might want in return.

"In the five months since the Esri found that gate, they've killed at least two dozen people and raped who knows how many more." Charlie's hand sliced upward. "And that's with one gate open. Now they've got all twelve unlocked...*and we don't know where they are.* We can't guard them. They'll have free rein of this world, enchanting and destroying at will. If we don't get those gates sealed, the human race is doomed. We can't wait, Harrison, and you know it."

Until five months ago, the humans hadn't known there *was* another world connected to theirs. In ancient times, the magical Esri had enchanted their human victims, raping virgins and stealing children to fill the slave halls and harems of Esria. Fifteen centuries ago, the Esrian princess, Ilaria, put a stop to the pillaging by sealing the known gates and leaving the keys, the seven stones of power, in the hands of the humans for safekeeping. Over the centuries, the humans had forgotten about the keys and all but forgotten about the creatures of Esria, most especially the Esri themselves—the pale, cruel, man-size beings who had once struck terror into every human heart. The terrifying tales evolved from generation to generation until the names the humans had once given the invaders, *faeries* and *elves,* were no longer whispered in terror but in joy and laughter.

The humans had never known that Ilaria had

left one gate unsealed, though hidden. And that the Esri had been searching for it ever since.

Five months ago, Tarrys's own master, Baleris, had stumbled upon the lost gate by accident—the first Esri to do so in fifteen centuries. She'd been with him, along with a second slave. Over the course of weeks, Baleris had found the strongest of the power stones, raped more than two dozen virgins, enchanted the entire D.C. police force, and hunted the humans he couldn't enchant, humans with a touch of blood from a long-ago Esri ancestor. Mortals whom the Esri called *Sitheen,* Charlie and Harrison among them. Baleris had rounded up dozens more virgins and had been preparing to take them back through the gate with him when the Sitheen stopped him, destroying him with fire and the ancient Esrian death chant.

With her master dead, Tarrys had finally been free. The humans had offered her sanctuary and she'd gladly accepted, but the other slave had escaped back into Esria to report to the Esrian king. Soon after, more Esri had come through the gate, and they'd found the seven stones, the seven keys, unlocking all the gates between the worlds.

The situation had quickly turned dire. And now Charlie Rand was determined to infiltrate Esria to find the one person who might be able to help them. The person who'd sealed the gates the first time.

Princess Ilaria.

Harrison silently watched his brother pace, his jaw working, clenching and unclenching. "At least take a guide. Take Tarrys."

Tarrys's pulse leaped with dismay, her fingers closing around her opposite wrist, her nails digging into her own tender flesh.

Charlie just snorted. "No way." He glanced at her, shooting her a quick, apologetic smile that nevertheless set hummingbirds to flight in her chest. "Nothing personal, eaglet, but you're safer here. And I'll make better time on my own."

Tarrys nodded. He didn't want her to go. She closed her eyes, waiting to savor the relief that should rush in at his words. But the relief wouldn't come. The truth remained—Esria was a magical and dangerous world and, no matter what he thought, Charlie Rand was ill-prepared to navigate it.

With help, *with her,* he might stand a chance.

Her heart thudded a hard, dull pounding. How could she turn her back on the only people who'd ever shown her kindness? The humans needed her help. They deserved what-ever aid she could give them. They had so much to lose if they failed to stop the Esri—their world, their *lives.*

In truth, she had nothing to lose. The free-dom and happiness she'd found here weren't real. They weren't hers. All her life she'd longed for the freedom to make her own deci-sions, to act as she chose instead of as another demanded. Now she finally had that freedom. The freedom to do what she knew was right.

How could she live with herself if, instead, she used her precious free will to hide?

Such a decision would not only be selfish, but

foolish. If the humans failed, the Esri would overrun the earth. Everything she'd found here, and everyone she'd come to care about, would be lost. Including her freedom.

Sweet Esria, can I really do this?

The fact that it was Charlie going made the decision both easier and infinitely harder. From their first meeting on the battlefield at the Dupont Circle Fountain, she'd had eyes for no one else. He was both strong and beautiful, warrior-hard, yet wonderfully gentle with those who weren't his enemy. She'd tried to kill him, yet he'd understood she was under Baleris's control, not her own, and had restrained her without hurting her. And her infatuation had bloomed.

He featured in all her dreams and was the focus of her desires, though she wished he wasn't. She resented even such a small loss of the precious control she'd finally claimed.

Fortunately Charlie didn't know his effect on her. He barely noticed her at all.

Her stomach clenched with dread at the

thought of what she must do. She slid her hand beneath the soft Redskins sweatshirt and pressed her fist against her warm abdomen, desperate to quiet the turmoil inside her.

Charlie didn't want her to come with him. Perhaps she could stay hidden, following him, watching over him, ready to intercede only if he needed her, only if he got into trouble. Until the Esri caught her and enslaved her again.

Charlie clasped his brother's shoulder. "Let's go. I'm sure Tarrys is ready for us to get out of here. And I need some sleep. I've got a mission to plan."

"This discussion isn't over," Harrison growled.

Charlie's expression turned to granite as he opened the door and ushered his brother through. "Yes. It is." The door clicked shut behind them.

Tarrys collapsed against the counter, her heartbeat fast and uneven, her mind awash in dread as she contemplated a future just like her past.

But, for now, all that mattered was remaining free long enough to keep Charlie Rand alive.

Charlie Rand loved a challenge.

There was nothing he enjoyed more than the rush of adrenaline before a dangerous op. But this particular op—infiltrating the unknown and dangerous world of Esria—unnerved even *his* steel-coated stomach. As he pushed through the door to the roof of Myrtle and Tarrys's apartment building that afternoon, Charlie realized that in less than ten hours, he would enter that strange world with no way to escape for a month. The gates between the worlds only opened during the midnight hour of a full moon.

Lying awake last night, he'd come to the conclusion he needed to polish his archery skills before he went through the gate. Not only were guns useless against the immortal Esri, but the sound was sure to draw unwanted attention. So he'd arranged a lesson from the finest archer he'd ever seen. The little Marceil, Tarrys.

He shook his head at the irony. Eight years as a navy SEAL, training with the most advanced weapons the world has ever known and what did he need? Bows and arrows.

Charlie buttoned his canvas jacket against the chill November breeze and headed around the brick structure that housed the stairs, following the sound of arrows zinging through the air. The first time he'd seen Tarrys, she'd been bald as a cue ball, dressed in some god-awful gray sack of a slave gown, and controlled by Baleris as that bastard prepared to herd several dozen young women through the gate. Baleris had ordered both Tarrys and his other slave to shoot the Sitheen, but even controlled, she'd managed to thwart the Esri and help the humans. She'd aimed and timed her arrow so perfectly, she'd knocked the other slave's arrow out of the air, leaving his intended victim untouched by either. An amazing shot.

Charlie didn't expect her to turn him into an Olympic-grade archer in a few hours. He just hoped she could fine-tune his own rudimentary technique and give him some tips on making his own equipment in that foreign world. Then he'd have weeks to practice shooting game so he could feed himself while he was in Esria.

"Tarrys?" Charlie called out, not wanting to startle her in the midst of firing a deadly weapon.

"Here." Her voice was clear and sure, surprising him a little. He'd always thought of her as meek, but maybe that wasn't fair considering he barely knew her. He'd been away from D.C. far more than he'd been here since Baleris found the gate. Though he tried to be in town for the full moon, other responsibilities demanded his time and attention. After his stint in the navy, he'd joined a civilian agency that did much the same kind of covert ops work without the political red tape. A couple weeks ago, he'd taken a leave of absence, finally devoting himself full-time to the Esri problem. If they didn't get these gates sealed, the rest of the world's troubles weren't going to matter.

Charlie turned the corner and for a second thought he'd come upon a stranger until he registered the slight stature and supershort hair of the shapely woman pulling arrows out of a target hung from the brick. He pulled up, watching her with interest and no small amount of surprise.

The snug jeans fit her perfectly, hugging her slender hips and falling just to the tops of her bare feet. Feet sporting pretty pink toenails. His admiring gaze rose to take in the clingy purple turtleneck that clung to a surprisingly ripe pair of breasts.

An appreciative smile tugged at his mouth. He'd always thought of her as cute in an alien, otherworldly kind of way. Like a buddy's violin-playing little sister or something. But there was nothing otherworldly about her today. No one would ever guess this woman wasn't human.

Until she glanced at him, revealing the most vibrant pair of violet eyes he'd ever seen.

"You look good, eaglet. I like the clothes."

Her gaze returned to the target as she pulled the last of the arrows. "Aunt Myrtle said I needed clothes that fit. I was fine with the others." Aunt Myrtle, the elderly aunt of one of the Sitheen, was a Sitheen herself and a gifted healer. She'd taken Tarrys under her wing while Tarrys looked after her in return.

Apparently, Myrtle had decided it was time to update Tarrys's wardrobe and replace the baggy T-shirts and sweatshirts she'd been wearing. He had to admit, the results were impressive.

"You liked those Redskins sweatshirts, huh?"

"They were soft."

Her simple words reminded him that she wasn't used to luxury. Hell, she'd been slave to one of the vilest creatures Charlie had ever encountered. Baleris. He couldn't begin to imagine what her life had been like. She deserved a little luxury.

"It looks like Myrtle's getting a start on your wardrobe. If there's anything else you need, you let me know, okay?"

He flashed her a smile as she glanced at him, but while her lips lifted gently, no answering smile reached her eyes. He sensed a sadness in those eyes he didn't remember seeing before, but he couldn't honestly say he'd ever noticed her eyes before, other than their arresting color. Maybe she was always sad.

Or maybe her melancholy had to do with his impending trip into Esria. If anyone knew the dangers he'd face there, it was Tarrys.

"You're not worrying about me, are you, eaglet? I'll be fine."

Her mouth compressed. "I'm concerned, yes. But I believe you'll succeed anyway."

He lifted a brow. "Is that a premonition talking? Any good news you want to share with me?"

A glimmer of a smile lit her eyes, and something else. Something he couldn't quite put his finger on. "I don't get premonitions." She slipped the bow on her shoulder with a shrug. "I have no magic. But I've watched you and heard the others talk about you. They believe that if anyone can succeed in freeing Princess Ilaria, you will. I agree."

He nodded slowly, watching her. "Thanks." But he'd heard her qualifier loud and clear. *If* anyone could.

There was something else, though he couldn't put his finger on it. He was getting a vibe from her that was slightly off, making his instincts itchy all of a sudden. Making him restless.

His gaze dropped, skimming the small, perfect proportion of her feminine body, and he had to admit that maybe it wasn't his instincts so much as his hormones kicking up that had him slightly on edge.

"Do you want to shoot first, or watch me?" Tarrys asked, dropping the handful of arrows into the quiver strapped to her back without looking, as if she'd been doing it all her life. She probably had. The flicker of challenge in her eyes definitely prodded his interest. He relaxed and grinned, not bothering to hide the subtle, surprising attraction he was feeling. "I want to watch you. Definitely want to watch you."

She met his gaze for the briefest instant before turning away, a hint of color in her cheeks, a small, charming smile on her lips.

Charlie smiled to himself as he followed her across the roof. She was as light-footed and graceful as a dancer and as proud and confident as any trained soldier. He'd never thought about it before—he'd never really spared any thought on the little Marceil at all—but she didn't cower or grovel as someone who'd been a slave. Probably because her masters had never had to break her spirit in order to control her. When the Esri enchanted a human, they controlled them body and mind. The human never knew what was happening. They never remembered. While the Esri couldn't take over a Marceil's mind, they could…and did… enslave their bodies, controlling every action with a thought or a touch.

Reaching the far end of the roof, Tarrys turned and met his gaze. "Do you want me to shoot slowly so you can see what I do, or normal speed?"

Charlie stepped out of her line of fire. "Normal speed. Show me what you've got." He studied her delicate profile as she faced the target, wondering why he'd never noticed how pretty she was. Her features were small—everything about her was small—but perfectly proportioned. Except, perhaps, her eyes, which were just about big enough to drown in. And that lower lip of hers, which was definitely full enough to catch his attention.

He shook his head and pried his gaze from her mouth. Her violet eyes flicked his way, unreadable, whispering of miles of untold depths. What was going on in that head of hers? He'd never before wondered, he realized. Never before noticed the gleam of sharp intelligence.

Too bad he was about to leave for Esria.

Without warning, Tarrys reached over her shoulder for an arrow, nocked and shot it, then reached for a second. He watched in stunned admiration as she fired six arrows in less than six seconds, hitting the target in a perfect line, top to bottom, alternating each arrow high and low.

A whoop of appreciation erupted from his throat. "Hot damn, eaglet. That was *brilliant.*"

He caught a glimpse of a smile on her mobile mouth before she handed him the bow. "Your turn."

Charlie laughed. "Yeah, right."

Her smile bloomed, amused and enchanting, then disappeared almost as quickly as it appeared, as if she were charmed by him and rather wished she weren't. And wasn't *that* an interesting thought? Yes, indeed, he loved a challenge.

"I'll get the arrows," she said.

His gaze followed her, watching her slender hips as she ran lightly across the roof. Reluctantly he tore his gaze away from her and focused on the target. A competitor by nature, and feeling a strange desire to impress, he was determined to make a good showing. As good as humanly possible.

Humanly possible, indeed.

Tarrys met him with the arrows and handed him one, not quite meeting his gaze. Charlie took a deep breath, nocked the arrow and drew the bow, then aimed and released. And watched the arrow land at the edge of the middle circle. Not bad, but…

"You're not holding it right," Tarrys said softly beside him.

He forced his pride down and met her gaze, seeing no smugness in her expression. "Show me."

She hesitated a moment, then closed the distance between them. The top of her head barely reached his shoulder as she pushed up the sleeves of her sweater, revealing delicate wrists and a thin, rustic wood bracelet.

"You're wearing holly," he said, surprised. Holly was the only thing known to protect humans from Esri enchantment. "I didn't know it worked on Marceils."

"I'm not sure it does," she admitted. "Larsen asked me to wear it anyway, just in case."

"Good idea."

Her scent teased his nostrils, sweet and crisp like some kind of exotic, forbidden fruit. But it was the touch of her slender fingers as she adjusted his grip that sent desire flaring sunbright inside him and blood surging between his legs.

Whoa. This was the little eaglet. The Sitheen's not-quite-human mascot. But his hormones couldn't have cared less.

Maybe Harrison was right. Maybe he *should* take her with him. She was a far better archer than he could ever hope to be. And he was surprisingly attracted to her, which might be kind of fun, if the feeling was mutual. But, no, he needed to move fast and quick and didn't need to be responsible for anyone, especially a tiny slip of a woman. Besides, it wouldn't be fair to ask her to go back there. She was safe here, and Myrtle relied on her.

Tarrys shifted her hands, bringing the inside of her wrist to rest on the back of his hand. He could feel her pulse racing like a raw recruit's before his first dive.

Hot damn.

But as his gaze dipped to her mouth, he noted the tenseness of her lips and suddenly wondered if her pulse raced from fear rather than attraction. The thought slammed into him hard. Of course it was fear. She'd been Baleris's slave, the slave of a rapist and murderer. Being this close to him…to any man… probably terrified her.

Hell.

"Now sight your target, imagine the flight of the arrow, and aim into it as you release." Her soft words flowed over him, echoing the thread of tension he'd felt in her, confirming his fears.

A pro at compartmentalizing, he forced himself to concentrate on the weapon and target. He pulled back the string and released the arrow. Just shy of a bull's-eye. Excellent.

"Good," Tarrys said, a smile in her voice. He

could feel her gaze on him and, while he still felt her tension, she hadn't moved away.

With a grin, he turned to her and found her watching him with a smile, and more, in her eyes. *Attraction.* So he wasn't wrong about that. But he wasn't entirely sure he was wrong about the fear either.

He resisted the temptation to probe deeper and explore this attraction a bit. Rule number one in the Charlie Rand Book of Dating clearly read, *Never date a woman you can't escape.* Tarrys lived with a Sitheen. When the relationship was over, there would be no getting away from her. And he owed her too much for her help with Baleris to do that.

There was something about Tarrys that was too innocent, too vulnerable for a casual affair and he didn't do anything deeper. No. Mutual attraction or not, this woman was a complication with a capital *C.* Good for a bit of flirtation and nothing more. The kind of woman no sane man went near unless he couldn't help himself. Unless he'd foolishly fallen head over heels in love.

And if there was one solid, immutable fact in life, it was this: *Charlie Rand didn't do love.*

Chapter 2

"Damn, Rand. You look like an Esri."

Jack Hallihan shook Charlie's hand as Jack and his wife, Larsen, joined Charlie a few minutes before midnight in front of the Dupont Circle Fountain. The cop and his wife, two of the small band of Sitheen, each carried a flamethrower, ready to defend the world against the Esri invaders when the gate opened in a few minutes.

"A little bigger than the last time I saw you, aren't you?" Larsen, an attractive blonde, patted Charlie's chest. "And lumpier. What in the world are you wearing under that outfit?"

Charlie grinned. The night was clear and brisk, a cold wind stinging his cheeks. He was dressed in the Esrian Royal Guard's uniform of silver tunic, black silk pants and black cloak. To the naked eye, he hoped to pass for an Esri. But beneath the costume, he was armed.

"Vest, T-shirt, and my gear." Everything from a first-aid kit to C-4 charges in case he needed to blow something open to reach the princess.

"You ready for this?" Jack asked.

Charlie shook his head. "Hell if I know." His breath fogged, glowing in the illumination from one of the streetlights. "How do you prepare for the twilight zone?"

He'd feel a hell of a lot better about this op if he could bring his team with him. Most of them were, like him, ex-SEALs. All had extensive special ops training. But he was the only one who had the trace of Esrian blood that made him immune to Esri enchantment. He'd seen Baleris turn the D.C. cops into his own personal army. The thought of an Esri turning his own men against him sent chills all the way to his toes.

Larsen gave him a hug and a kiss on the cheek. "Be careful, Charlie. We need you back."

"I'll be fine." He wasn't sure if he said the words to convince her or himself. "Where's Tarrys? I thought you were bringing her."

Larsen glanced to his right. "She stopped to talk to Harrison."

Charlie turned and saw Tarrys heading toward them. Not the attractive petite who'd stirred his hormones this afternoon, but once more the Marceil slave, complete with gray sacklike slave gown, two bows slung over one shoulder and a pair of quivers on her back.

What the hell?

A growl of frustration rumbled in his throat. Harrison was behind this. His brother was the most controlling son of a bitch on the planet.

And Tarrys was playing his game. He stalked toward her. "I already told you, you're not coming with me," he snapped.

Tarrys stopped short, her expression filling with a wariness that bordered on fear.

Charlie caught himself, reining in his temper. "I'm not mad, eaglet. I'm not mad at *you,* anyway." He stopped an arm's length in front of her, glad to see she didn't back away. Once again, she looked a little otherworldly. Until his gaze dropped to the hand holding the two bows, fingernails painted pink. That pink nail polish reminded him that the woman in the purple sweater and snug jeans was still in there. Her sweet scent wafted over him, heating his blood, driving home the lesson. Even dressed like Friar Tuck she stirred his interest.

She met his gaze without flinching. "You can't go through the gate alone, Charlie Rand."

"Yeah, I know that." Humans didn't possess the magical genes to get through without an escort from Esria. "But all you have to do is hand me through, right? You don't actually have to go all the way through yourself."

"I don't have to stay, but I have to go through." Her gaze broke from his and traveled to the mammoth fountain that was the location of the gate into Esria. "I will go first, then come back for you." Her gaze slowly returned to his. "I would not have you walk into a trap."

His gut started crawling and he looked at her sharply. "Do you have reason to believe there's a trap waiting for me?"

Her eyes widened. "No. But as I've told you, I don't have the gift of foreknowledge. If there are Esri in the area, I'll draw less attention if I'm dressed properly."

"If there are Esri in the area..." A chill washed over him at the thought. She'd be snatched and enslaved and there'd be no one there to protect her. "Forget it. We're going through together. If we find Esri waiting for us, we'll come right back."

There was something about the little Marceil that brought out his protective instincts. Her size probably had something to do with it. But it was more than that. He'd seen her under the control of Baleris, seen the way she fought against the son of a bitch's far superior power.

And he knew she'd probably suffered serious abuse at the bastard's hands. No way could he blithely let her go back to that.

She'd take him through the gate and come right back. Nothing more.

"The gate's open." Kade's voice resonated over the park.

Charlie's pulse leaped as he lifted his flame-thrower and ran to take his place with the others. There were five of them guarding the gate tonight, four Sitheen and Kade.

Harrison stood on Charlie's right. Jack and Larsen had taken up position across the park, on the other side of the fountain. And on Charlie's left stood Kade, seven feet of hard-muscled immortal. Kade didn't look Esrian, especially in his jeans and leather jacket. He'd been as surprised as the rest of them when they'd realized he was only half Esri. It turned out that both his parents, born more than fifteen centuries ago, were half human, but Kade had inherited his dad's dark hair and Caucasian skin and his mom's immortality.

The Sitheen were more than happy to have him on their side.

He'd lived fifteen centuries in Esria until a month ago when he'd stolen through the gate on a mission to destroy the Sitheen and steal back the strongest of the seven stones. When he'd realized the full extent of his king's evil plans for the human race, he'd discovered he had too much humanity in him to let it happen. It hadn't hurt that he'd fallen in love with a human—Larsen's friend, Autumn.

As he stood by the fountain, Charlie saw that the light of the full moon had cast the three life-size statues carved into the fountain's pedestal into ghostly relief. The statues looked ready to leap naked from the marble.

Charlie settled his flamethrower securely in both hands. Adrenaline pumped through his veins like rocket fuel. Within the next sixty minutes, he'd be walking through that gate himself. But first, he had to help make sure no Esri jumped out.

A chill breeze molded the silk pants against

Charlie's legs and lifted the hem of his borrowed cloak. He was wearing Kade's uniform from the Esrian Royal Guard. The uniform had been hastily altered to fit his more normal, six-one frame. With any luck, if he did run into Esri he could pass himself off as a mixed blood immortal, like Kade. If they figured out he was mortal, he was dead.

Charlie glanced at the giant. "Any last-minute advice before I go through?"

"Stay away from the Esri," Kade advised.

Charlie laughed. "Yeah, I figured that much. Anything else?"

"No. Nothing that I haven't already told you. Other than the Esri, the biggest threat to you are the black trimors, but there's not a lot you can do about them except hope you don't cross their paths. You'll never see them coming."

"Great." If there wasn't anything he could do about them, he wasn't going to worry about them.

He'd spent all morning with Kade, learning as much as he could about the place—what to eat, what to avoid, like the deadly, cat-like black trimors that remained invisible until the moment of attack. And how to reach the Forest of Nightmares where Princess Ilaria had been held captive for more than three hundred years. Kade knew she was alive. Linked by the magic of their world, all Esri knew the moment one of their own died…and at whose hands. Princess Ilaria still lived.

But rescuing her was going to be a feat of gigantic proportions and Kade could offer no advice. He'd never been in the Forest of Nightmares. No Esri entered those dark woods willingly.

"I wish I could go with you," Kade said, sounding frustrated.

Charlie couldn't imagine what the man was feeling. Just last night Kade had killed one of his own men as that Esri forced open the gate a day early and tried to abscond with the seven stones of power that were the keys to the gates…and so much more. Kade had stopped him but at a terrible cost. It was forbidden to end an immortal life, and Kade was now marked for death should he ever return to Esria. The moment he stepped through one of the gates, every Esri would know and be able to track him. They would terminate his existence long before he got anywhere near the Forest of Nightmares.

Now Kade was stuck here and Charlie was going into Esria alone.

Silence settled over the small group as they watched the fountain, waiting. The tension in Charlie's gut twisted even as adrenaline simmered in his veins. Fifteen minutes. Thirty. Forty-five. *Enough.*

He stepped forward, breaking the circle. "If they were coming through, they'd have done it by now. I can't wait any longer."

One by one, the others left their positions to shake his hand and wish him luck.

Finally, Harrison stepped up to him. Charlie had never gotten along well with his too-serious older brother. But this wasn't the time for old fights. And he had a sense of what it was costing Harrison to watch him enter the Esrian world. Harrison's first experience with the Esri had been a nightmare. He'd taken his young kids to the Kennedy Center to see *The Lion King* and fallen victim to Baleris instead. Baleris had done no more than touch Harrison's six-year-old daughter, Stephie, for an instant, but the pain he'd launched into her small body had damaged her in ways no doctor could repair. Even Aunt Myrtle, with her gift for healing, hadn't been able to help her. Months later, the child still remained catatonic and might stay that way for the rest of her life.

Anger flared every time he thought of his little niece, but Charlie knew his anger was nothing compared to his brother's. Harrison hated the Esri with a depth that was chilling. He wouldn't deal well with the loss of a second family member to that evil.

But Charlie had every intention of making it back alive. He grinned to lighten the mood. "Cheer up, Harrison. I'm going to kick some major Esri butt."

Harrison's cool expression never wavered. "If I don't hear from you in a month, I'm coming in after you."

Charlie scowled. "Stay the hell away, Harrison, I mean it." If *he,* a trained special operative, couldn't handle Esria, what chance did his white-collar CEO of a brother stand? "I'll try to make it back in a month, but it might take longer and I can't exactly call to give you an update. I've got at least several weeks of walking ahead of me just to reach the freakin' forest. After that, who knows how long it'll take to free the princess and find another gate out of there. Just stay put until I get back."

Charlie clasped his brother's shoulder. "I *will* come back, Harrison. I promise." He forced himself to smile again. "With a fairy princess on my arm."

Harrison snorted, the faintest hint of a smile twitching his lips. "Get your cocky ass through that gate, little brother."

Their gazes held as something heavy passed

between them. The knowledge that this might be goodbye.

Charlie refused to accept that. "Keep an eye on the apartment for me." He turned to look for Tarrys and found her waiting quietly behind him. "You ready, eaglet?"

She nodded and held out her hand to him.

"Be careful, both of you," Larsen called as Charlie's fingers closed around the surprising warmth of Tarrys's fine-boned hand. Excitement sparked inside him, adrenaline charging through his system as it always did at the start of an op.

Charlie glanced down at the delicate profile of his pretty companion. "Let's do this."

Her face lifted and she met his gaze, her eyes shining like violet-hued silver in the moonlight, piercing him with their intensity, stirring that excitement.

"Be safe, Charlie Rand."

His gaze dropped to that intriguing mouth of hers and for half a second he thought about kissing her. And wouldn't that give the others something to talk about when he was gone?

But before he could give it another thought, Tarrys turned and tugged him with her as she stepped onto the fountain's rim and down into the dry well. When they reached the thick marble pedestal, Charlie hesitated. Tarrys didn't. Inch by inch, she disappeared until all but her hand was gone…the hand caught tight in his.

Then she gave a tug and pulled him into chaos.

Charlie opened his eyes to a canopy of spinning, glowing orange, confusion clouding his mind.

Where was he? What had happened? His mind scrambled for an answer as he quickly took stock of the situation. He was on his back, something hard pinned beneath him. No pain. So he was either unhurt or so close to dead nothing mattered.

Something entered his line of vision, flying about twenty feet above him. *What the...?*

A snake. A green-and-white-striped snake with long black wings.

In a dizzying rush, it all came back.

Esria. Chills raced across his flesh.

Charlie blinked, stayed where he was a moment longer, listening for sound. When none met his ears, he slowly glanced in every direction, wanting to make sure there was no obvious reason to stay down. The familiar smells of loam and pine mixed with a flowery-metallic scent that burned his nostrils.

The alien landscape that caught his gaze made his heart stutter. It was as if he'd stumbled into a cartoon world where the artist had mixed up all the colors. The light was dim, but not dark, the sky low, glowing like a dark orange dome over a colorful yet barren terrain. A few clumps of straggly trees or bushes and a scattering of jewel-colored rocks were all that relieved the hilly expanse of blue, *royal* blue, dirt. Except for the small patch of vibrant pink flowers he'd managed to land upon.

He sat up, then slowly rose to his feet, adjusting the bow and quiver slung over his shoulder, his senses alert, his gaze searching for sign of trouble. But the land was utterly quiet. He was alone.

Tarrys.

His gaze searched for her even as he knew she wouldn't still be here. A tiny regret had him wishing he'd at least had a moment to say goodbye. Maybe he could have snagged himself a kiss for good luck.

Right.

Sounds began to rise around him, sounds he'd probably silenced with his arrival. Insects, if he had to guess, but unlike any he'd ever heard before—odd clicks, musical screeches, and a host of others, pitched both high and low. He hoped to God they were merely insects and not something that might decide to put him on the dinner menu.

A chill slid down his spine, part excitement,

part reaction to the total unknown. What dangers lurked in this place that he might never know existed until too late?

With a start, he realized the flowers had disappeared. All that remained beneath his feet was a tuft of orange-and-gold grass.

Jesus.

He looked around, trying to get his bearings, needing to figure out which way to go. Where was the gate? His gut clenched with the sharp realization that it didn't matter. Even if he stayed here and waited for the gate to open in a month, he couldn't get through. Not without help. There was no turning back. The only way he'd ever get home was hand in hand with the princess herself. Anything less and he'd never see home again.

Which was precisely the reason he wouldn't fail.

Determination surged into the flow of adrenaline firing his body and he grinned. God, he loved a challenge. But as he looked for his first landmark, the twin peaks of the red mountains, a sound reached his ears, beneath the clicks and squeals of the night creatures, that had ice forming in his blood.

The sound of voices. Human voices.

No, not human.

Esri.

Chapter 3

Charlie tensed, his mind scrambling as he listened to the low, unintelligible voices drawing nearer. Esri voices. From the sound of them, they were just below the rise, less than twenty yards away. Three Esri, he'd guess. Maybe four. By the time he knew for sure, they'd be able to see him. And he couldn't kill them, unfortunately. He *might* be able to outrun them, but a human-looking Royal Guard running from the gate was going to look damned suspicious. No, the only thing to do was hide and pray none of them possessed a gift that would sense him. He scanned the area and spied a nearby thicket of low, bloodred bushes that might do the trick. It would have to. Using skills honed as a SEAL, he ran across the hard-packed dirt to the bushes without making a sound. As he ducked low within the center of the soft, fuzzy branches, a flurry of winged insects took to the air, like a spray of raindrops flying skyward.

Wishing for some red camouflage paint, Charlie took a deep breath and concentrated on quieting his thudding heart. Calm. Steady. He looked back the way he'd come and nearly had a heart attack. A narrow path of that same thick rust-and-gold grass led straight to him. Grass that hadn't been there a moment ago, as if it had followed him. It was going to lead them right to him!

The grass disappeared.

Charlie blinked. Shit. Nothing remained of the grass except the tuft beneath his feet. He reached down to feel the stuff and had gotten nothing more than the fleeting impression that it felt like the grass at home when the grass disappeared and he once more found himself on a bed of tiny pink flowers.

Charlie's skin raced with goose bumps. Kade had warned him that the two worlds didn't follow the same laws of nature. He'd laugh at the understatement if he weren't quite so shaken.

The nearing voices pulled his attention away from the insta-garden beneath his feet and again he prayed none of the Esri possessed the ability to sense his energy. While every Esri had certain baseline abilities, each had unique gifts as well. Hell, most of their human descendants...the Sitheen...did too, with the unfortunate exception of his own line. Neither he nor Harrison had any special talents except for the inability to be enchanted which, all things considered, was really all that mattered.

Still, it would have been nice to have had some magic at his disposal. Larsen foresaw death. Jack could speak with his Sitheen ancestors. Myrtle was a healer of prodigious skill. The Esri, Baleris, had been able to smell the power stones. And Zander, the Esri Kade had killed, had been able to sense power in others.

If any of the approaching Esri possessed *that* ability, he was in trouble. Because if they could smell power, even the low-level power of a human's life force, they'd know he was here.

Pale heads broke the level of the rise. Charlie watched, barely breathing, as three male Esri wearing the same silver tunics and black cloaks he himself wore came fully into view. One of the three possessed the startling whiteness of both hair and skin that he'd come to associate with true Esri, but the other two just looked deathly pale. All three were fairly tall with lanky, rangy builds. Their hair varied in shade from stark white to white-blond.

Though the air temperature was comfortable, a trickle of sweat rolled down Charlie's neck as the trio neared, speaking Esrian gibberish. If they caught him, he was going to have to decide whether to run or grunt and thump his chest and hope they backed off, though why they'd be afraid of someone who'd been hiding in the bushes, he couldn't fathom.

The Esri neared, their voices growing louder. Clearer. With a jolt, Charlie realized he was starting to understand snatches of what they were saying. "…gate…nearby…" "…must have closed…" "…King Rith…displeased."

Goose bumps rippled over his skin. He was beginning to understand *Esrian*. Had he inherited a gift from his Esri ancestor after all? Or was this newfound ability just part of the magic of this world? Kade had warned him to expect anything. He'd been expecting the worst, but speaking the language was a huge plus.

"We are not even certain the gate is here," said the shortest and whitest of the three Esri.

"I felt it." The speaker's face was rounder, his hair thick with straw-blond waves. "When it opens again, I will know."

The first man made a noise of dismay. "That won't happen for another cycle."

"So we wait."

Charlie gave a mental groan. Don't wait *here*. If they settled in, he was sunk.

But the men never stopped, never glanced his way, just continued to walk toward the hills. Finally, when they were but a speck on the horizon, Charlie crept out of the bushes and headed the other way.

He was being followed.

Charlie picked up his pace as he crossed the rocky, hilly blue terrain, the rust-and-gold grass appearing beneath his feet with every step and disappearing a few steps behind him. The grass had entertained him for a while after he escaped the Esri at the gate.

He'd been so distracted by the grass, he hadn't noticed when he'd first picked up the tail.

The trees had grown more numerous the farther he traveled from the gate, thin patches of woods cropping up here and there, the trees resembling those in his world only in their basic shape. They had trunks and branches and leaves. But the trunks were blue or green or some combination, some shimmery as satin, others spiked with thorns. And the leaves looked like an autumn forest with the color turned up two hundred percent. Reds, golds, oranges as bright as crayons from a coloring box.

Unfortunately, scattered everywhere were bushes and rocks as big as boulders. Whoever was following him had plenty of places to hide.

Charlie followed the stream Kade had told him would lead him through the mountains. It wasn't the most direct route, but would provide him with water the entire journey. A necessity, especially since large bodies of water were rare in Esria.

In the distance rose the twin red peaks he knew he'd have to cross. The air was cool and comfortable with a light breeze that brushed his heated skin—skin heated from exertion and the tension of feeling he had a bull's-eye painted on his back. He didn't dare confront his stalker unless he had no choice.

Nearly two hours had passed since he'd tumbled through the gate, more than an hour since he'd caught a glimpse of movement and felt the familiar sensation of being watched. But he'd yet to see the man who followed. Or hear him.

Damn, but he hated being without his team. In any other op, one of his men would slip away and double back to spy on the spy. But he was stuck. As soon as his pursuer knew he'd been made, he might no longer hang back. Which meant a confrontation Charlie couldn't afford. But neither could he go on like this indefinitely. Sooner or later he'd need sleep. Better to confront him and try to scare the hell out of him while he could. *If* he could.

But first, he wanted to see his tail and make certain there was only one.

It took three tries, slipping behind bushes or trees before he finally caught a glimpse of the one following him as he darted from one boulder to another high on the hill above him. A Marceil, if the small size and gray gown were anything to go by. But this Marceil had hair. Very short, dark hair.

Tarrys.

Relief hit him first and hard, relief that he didn't have an Esri on his tail. Anger followed fast on its heels.

Damn her. He'd *told* her in no uncertain terms she wasn't coming with him. Was this her doing or Harrison's? It didn't matter now. But, yeah, it did. If this was her doing and she hadn't told anyone she was planning to stay in Esria, the others would assume they'd been captured. Harrison would jump through the gate at the next full moon to fulfill the mission he would assume Charlie had already failed.

Dammit.

His jaw clenched, his eyes burrowing beneath his brows as he fought to hide the telltale signs of emotion. The first thing he intended to do was lure her to him so he could wring her delicate little neck. The second was send her away, somewhere safe to spend the next month until the gate opened again. If he'd wanted her company, he'd have asked for it.

Fisting his hands on his knees, he straightened and resumed walking as if nothing was wrong. For a moment, he considered trying to outdistance himself from her, but he didn't know what kind of stamina she had. Besides, allowing her to follow him was too dangerous. If he picked up a second tail…a *true* threat…he might not realize it until it was too late.

Damn her. If she thought she could thwart him and get away with it, she was dead wrong.

Tarrys ducked behind a crystalberry bush, the sound of its fruit jangling like broken glass in the dull breeze. Peering around it, she watched Charlie, his long strides carrying him quickly toward the foothills of the red mountains. She ran, dodging behind a boulder, then another bush, determined to stay close enough to watch him. Determined that he not see her in return.

Sweat rolled between her breasts and dampened her scalp as she struggled to stay hidden and keep him in sight. They'd only come through the gate a few hours ago and already she was tiring of this. Eventually, Charlie would rest. Then and only then would she catch her breath.

She'd planned to run from Charlie when they first came through the gate, at least until the gate closed and he could no longer send her back. But the shift between the worlds had knocked him unconscious, giving her the perfect opportunity to hide.

Then the Esri arrived and she'd been terrified the mission would be over before it began. She'd been prepared to draw them off, giving Charlie a chance to get away. But Charlie had moved fast and the Esri had passed, unaware.

Now the only things chasing her were memories, and the fear that an Esri would catch her before she saw Charlie safely across Esria.

She scanned the surrounding hills, looking for a sign of others. Few traveled these lands. The chances of crossing paths with one was unlikely, but not nearly unlikely enough. The thought of it stirred the fear that had ridden over her like a haze since her return.

Sweet Esria, she didn't want to be back here. Walking through that gate had been, without doubt, the hardest thing she'd ever done. If not for Charlie's hand clasped hard around hers, giving her strength, reminding her of her purpose, she wasn't sure she'd have been able to force her feet into that fountain. Every step since, she'd felt fate's hot breath on the back of her neck, corralling her toward that awful and inevitable moment of capture and enslavement.

Don't think about the past. Don't think about the future. Charlie. Only Charlie. And getting him safely over the mountains. That was all that mattered. All she could allow herself to think about, or she'd go slowly mad.

Yet she couldn't stop the wish that she'd never gone into the human realm in the first place. That she'd never known freedom or kindness. Or friendship. How much easier her future years would be had she never known what it was like to have someone speak to her as an equal. To feel the touch of a friendly hand. To laugh and to do as she wanted knowing her body was hers to command. To know that no one would draw her into a frenzy of false passion for the purpose of raping her.

That the only desire that stirred inside her was drawn by a man who didn't mean to attract her as he did. And Charlie would never, she was certain, force himself upon her.

And while she'd prefer to not be attracted to him, or any man, the truth was she liked him. A lot. Far more than she wanted to. He was a good man. A man who'd shown her more simple kindness than any man had since she was a child.

For Charlie and Aunt Myrtle and all the humans she'd begun to care for, she would do what she could to make sure Charlie succeeded. She would do what she must.

She peered around the edge of the rock, watching, staking out her next hiding spot. But as her gaze swung back to Charlie, she saw him stumble, then fall to his knees, swaying as if he'd been arrow shot. Her jaw dropped, shock vibrating through her body as she watched the strong warrior collapse slowly onto his back as if in the throes of human death.

No.

Heart thundering in her chest, Tarrys darted out from behind the rock and ran down the rocky hillside, the grass rising to prick her feet as fear congealed into a hard mass deep in her throat.

"Charlie." His name was little more than a breath as she reached him and fell to her knees beside him. "Charlie, wake up." But her hands had barely brushed his tunic when his own snapped up to capture her wrists.

Tarrys strangled a scream as the man she'd thought unconscious sat up then leaped to his feet, dragging her with him, his eyes blazing.

"What are you doing here?"

He wasn't injured at all. It was a ruse to catch her. Her knees nearly buckled with relief. "You knew I was following you."

"Of course I knew you were following me. I've known for miles."

The day hadn't even broken and already her plan was ruined.

Anger washed off him in waves, yet she didn't fear him. Her heart pounded only from his startling her. And from the storming of her senses by his nearness. Sweet Esria, she was falling under his enchantment all over again.

He gave her arms a shake. "Answer me. Why did you come?"

"To protect you."

Charlie gave a short bark of laughter, but there was no humor in the sound, nor in the hard twist of his mouth. He held her so close she could smell his uniquely masculine scent, as deep, rich and endlessly fascinating as his world. His grip on her wrists was no more than snug, yet her skin burned where he touched her. Burned not with pain but with a heat that sank beneath her flesh, into the heart of her blood. Inciting a desire she wanted to feel for no man.

Her body's reaction frustrated her. Charlie's belief in his own invulnerability…and her uselessness…annoyed her. "There are things about my world you don't know," she snapped.

"I'm not denying that, but I don't need a freakin' babysitter." He shook her again, the tension in his hands tightly…barely…controlled. "And you left the others thinking… what? That I was dead? Captured?"

"No!" Her gaze snapped up to meet his. "Harrison knew I was staying with you." As Charlie's expression darkened even more, she added quickly, "He didn't ask me to come. This was my decision. But I told him before we left."

"I'm sure you made him obscenely happy with that news," he said disgustedly.

"He thought it was a good idea."

"I'll bet he did. He's not the one that has to…" He released her suddenly. "You can't come with me."

Tarrys said nothing, unable to agree yet unwilling to lie. If he chased her away, she'd only go back to following him, though how she'd keep him from seeing her this time, she couldn't fathom. She'd been so careful!

"Go home, Tarrys. Or somewhere you'll be safe. Or, better yet, find someplace around here to hole up for a few weeks until that gate opens again. Keep out of sight. Even if Esri go through the gate at the next full moon, Harrison and the others will be there. They'll protect you."

As she remained silent, his stiffness softened ever so slightly. "Look, eaglet, I appreciate your trying to help, though…*Jesus*…I can't believe you put yourself in danger to come after me. But you'll slow me down. This mission is time-critical and I've got to move fast."

The gentling of his attitude softened something deep inside her. As much as she longed to stop her body's reaction to this man, she would never be able to harden her heart toward him.

"I know," she said simply.

His gaze sharpened on her, his eyes probing hers, as if he sought a way into her innermost thoughts. When they narrowed, honed to a piercing point, she thought maybe he had.

Charlie scowled. "If I try to send you away, you'll just follow me again, won't you?"

Tarrys pursed her lips. If he were anyone else, she'd consider lying to him. But she was beginning to think there was no hiding from Charlie Rand. Whether in actions or words.

She met his gaze. "Your mission is to free Princess Ilaria. Mine is to make sure you succeed. I won't give up mine any more than you will yours."

Charlie scowled. "Harrison *did* put you up to this."

"No. No one did. This was my plan. My choice."

"It's not your *mission* if you make it up on your own."

She cocked her head. "Who directed you to free Princess Ilaria?" She couldn't believe her temerity in questioning him like this. A few months ago, she never would have dared question any man, *anyone,* but the humans had encouraged her to speak freely. She'd embraced that freedom more slowly but no less appreciatively than the others.

And this was Charlie. For a reason she couldn't fully understand, she knew he'd never hurt her, no matter what she said or did.

"My going after Princess Ilaria is different. It needs to be done." His eyes snapped with determination as his gaze held hers.

Tarrys lifted her chin. "And you need to reach her safely. Doing all I can to make that happen is what *I* have to do." She suddenly couldn't bear having him so unhappy with her. Looking into his eyes, she implored him to understand, and reached for him, only to let her hand drop to her side. "I've never been free to choose my path before, Charlie. And I won't remain so forever. While I can, I choose to help the humans win. And that means making sure you succeed."

He watched her for breathless moments, his gaze delving deep inside her, stirring her pulse and her own determination.

Finally, he looked up at the sky that was beginning to lighten to a soft gold. Twining his fingers behind his head, he arched back, squeezing his eyes closed as if he were in pain.

With a groan, he straightened and looked at her, his expression wry but not unkind. "You're a stubborn little thing, aren't you? If you're coming, you're going to have to keep up. I can't slow down for you. There's too much at stake."

"I understand."

Something gleamed in his eyes she couldn't quite name. A challenge, perhaps? He wasn't going to make this easy on her. But she didn't expect him to. Didn't *want* him to. She'd come to help him, not slow him down. But she had to wonder how much more difficult this journey was going to be on her now that she'd consigned herself to his side night and day.

Charlie turned and started off again, his strides longer, if possible, than before.

With a sigh, Tarrys held tight to her bow with one hand, lifting the hem of her gown with her other, and hurried after him.

Though she trusted him never to hurt her physically, she feared he'd end up hurting her all the same, more than any Esri ever could.

The woman was tireless.

All day Charlie had kept up this pace, driving them both hard and fast for more than twelve hours, resting for no more than minutes at a time. He'd been certain she wouldn't last. Certain that she'd suddenly remember someplace else she could go to wait for the gate to open again. But he was damn near exhausted and Tarrys still jogged at his side.

They'd yet to see another person, thankfully, but he'd gotten an eyeful of the local wildlife. They'd watched a herd of white deer with large red polka dots leap over the stream as lightly as Santa's reindeer taking off. The flying snakes with their high-pitched screams were everywhere, wrapping themselves around high tree branches when they lighted. But the ones he'd found the most interesting, if oddly unsettling, were the packs of neon-green chipmunks that scurried across the ground like large shag rugs on the move.

Charlie hazarded a glance behind him where Tarrys followed close. Sweat glistened on her forehead, but her expression showed no sign of distress.

The little slave was tougher than she looked.

At first, her stubbornness had annoyed him. Hell, everything about this situation annoyed him. But he couldn't help admiring the courage it had taken to give up the cushy life she had now to try to make a difference. But *wanting* to help wasn't the same thing as helping. He couldn't afford to compromise his mission just to make her feel good about herself. He wasn't giving an inch. Either she kept up, or she found somewhere to hide until the gates opened again.

Tarrys wasn't his problem.

He couldn't afford to let her be, though he had to keep stirring his anger to keep the need to protect her at bay.

* * *

"Tarrys, wake up. It's time to get going."

Tarrys groaned silently, her exhausted body crying at the thought of rising, of moving at all, let alone returning to that bone-jarring run she'd had to maintain to keep up with Charlie's much longer strides. She felt like she'd just closed her eyes. And probably had.

The rogue thought flitted through her mind that she could tell him to go on without her. To let her sleep. But helping the humans was the only useful thing, the only *real* thing, she'd ever done. Nothing would stop her. Nothing short of enslavement.

The slightly caustic smell of the pink flower beds teased her nostrils, the air filled with the clicking sounds of the night insects. Her eyes opened, heavy and coarse with grit. The sky was starting to lighten again, but they'd traveled most of the night. They couldn't have rested for any time at all.

Charlie stood over her, looking tired but utterly determined. He didn't have to say the

words for her to hear them ringing in her head.
You have to keep up.

She forced herself to her feet and slung her
bow and quiver over her shoulder. When he
turned and strode off in that ground-eating gait
of his, she once more ran, though her body felt
like it was going to come apart and start dropping, piece by piece onto the ground. Marceils
healed injuries quickly, but she needed rest and
sleep to replenish her stores of energy. And
she'd had little of either in more than a day.

None of that mattered. Nothing but staying
with Charlie Rand, though she wondered what
use she'd be to him if all she could do now was
to keep one foot moving in front of the other.

"We're on a collision course with a chipmunk
rug," Charlie said a short while later. "Should
we step aside and let them pass?"

"No." She caught a glimpse of green, but
could see little beyond Charlie's broad back.
"They'll go around us."

Minutes later, several hundred small green
petermoles covered the ground at their feet.

Charlie stopped so quickly, Tarrys nearly ran into him.

"You can keep walking," she told him, though the respite was welcome. "You can't step on them."

"That's not why I stopped. I swear I just saw a big black cat with three white horns. But it disappeared almost as quickly as it appeared."

Tarrys froze. Her blood went cold.

"*A black trimor.* The most deadly creature in Esria."

Chapter 4

Tarrys grabbed his arm. "Get behind me! A black trimor will kill you."

"Like hell." Charlie pulled his knife as he stared at the sea of neon-green, watching as another chipmunk levitated into the air. For an instant…only an instant…a catlike creature about the size of a German shepherd, black with three white horns sticking out of his forehead, appeared to eat the little guy. Then both disappeared. "I'm really seeing him, right?"

"Yes. They're invisible until they snatch their prey…or attack. And there's more than one." She stepped away from him and lifted her bow. "I see four. Tell me if you see more."

Four? He felt as if his eyes were playing tricks on him, but yeah, now that she mentioned it, he was seeing things in his peripheral vision—a flash of black appearing for a second, then disappearing.

Beside him, Tarrys began shooting, arrow after arrow. He thought about doing the same, but knew she had the best chance of striking one of those creatures.

Her movements were swift and graceful, edged with a desperation that did little to reassure him as she spun, shooting in every direction. They were surrounded, the trimors working at the edges of the chipmunk rug. But the black trimors never stayed visible long enough for one of Tarrys's arrows to hit its mark. Charlie wondered if he'd have been more effective with a gun, but doubted it. By the time he saw the creatures, they were gone.

"Got one!" Tarrys crowed even as she continued to shoot. The one she'd shot fell, an arrow through one eye. A moment later, it disappeared.

"Charlie, I'm nearly out of arrows. I'll need your quiver."

He pulled it off his back and waited, handing it to her the moment she shot the last arrow from her own. With remarkable grace, she dropped the first and slung the second quiver onto her back, the arrows flying in an almost fluid continuity.

A second cat went down with an arrow through the neck, followed by Tarrys's chilling words.

"I'm out of arrows."

"Back to back," he ordered. Though what good it would do when they couldn't see the creatures, he wasn't sure. "Unless you have a better idea?"

"A trimor paralyzes its larger prey, or its enemies, by goring them with its central horn and pumping them full of poison. Neither the goring nor the poison will automatically kill me. They will you. While I draw their attack—"

"No way."

Tarrys continued as if he hadn't spoken. "—you kill them with your knife. You'll have to be fast."

"They could still kill you." Her plan went against every instinct he possessed.

She met his gaze, violet eyes flashing with steely determination. "If we're not very quick and very lucky, they're going to kill us both. I may heal fast, but even I can't survive being eaten."

Dammit. His pride protested, but he took a deep breath and forced it aside. She might be small and female, but she was all warrior and this might be the only chance they got. They were going to do this together or not at all.

"How will you draw their attack when you can't see them?"

"Noise. Stay close behind me."

As Tarrys lunged forward with a high-pitched scream, Charlie followed. Sure enough, a moment later a cat appeared, in full leap, his head down. Before Charlie could react, that long, razor-sharp center horn gored Tarrys clean through the chest.

Charlie went berserk. Horror screamed through him as he flew at the cat, digging his knife deep in the creature's throat, ripping through muscle and sinew. Warm blood spurted from the animal, mixing with the blood that bloomed on Tarrys's gown. The cat fell, taking Tarrys with it, fully impaled on its horn.

As he reached for her, the second cat appeared, leaping for him. His fury found an outlet and lent speed to his reflexes as he shoved his knife upward into the attacking cat's jaw, lodging it deep in the animal's skull. That deadly center horn caught on the fabric of his tunic, but didn't break through.

Close. Too close.

The cat fell dead at his feet then disappeared a second later, leaving his knife lying, bloody, on the ground.

He snatched the knife and crouched, watching for more cats. But the green carpet had passed them by and nothing else moved.

Finally he whirled back to Tarrys and knelt beside her, turning her gently onto her back. The trimor gone, she now lay on a bed of dark pink flowers as if she'd been laid out for burial. A bloom of blood the size of his palm covered her chest. And her eyes, those vibrant, violet eyes, stared at nothing, unblinking, her expression frozen in a mask of pain. *A mask of death.*

Charlie felt as if he'd been sucker punched, his heart skipping a beat, then racing faster than it had during the attack.

Tarrys was dead.

No. Not dead. Paralyzed. Wasn't she? How in the hell was he supposed to know?

Lifting her hand, he pressed it between his own. Her flesh was warm and damp, the perfection marred by a faint green allover mottling, but that hardly told him anything. She could still be dead.

The thought went through him like a blade. She'd saved his life. If he'd come upon this scenario alone, it would be him lying on that bed of flowers. And he *would* be dead.

"Can you hear me, eaglet?"

No response, but he hadn't really expected one. "I should have asked you how long the paralysis lasts. Or, hell, if there's something I need to do to bring you out of it." This place was filled with magic. What if the poison wasn't a toxin so much as a curse? What if she was like Sleeping Beauty or something?

Charlie stared at her, at those lips parted with pain. What did he have to lose? It wasn't like kissing her was any kind of hardship.

He leaned over and pressed his lips to hers. Her scent filled his nostrils. Even totally unresponsive, she moved him, the feel of her damp mouth beneath his stirring something warm and exciting inside him.

When she didn't respond, he pulled back and studied her, searching her eyes.

"It was worth a try," he said with a shrug.

Something flickered in her eyes.

He squeezed her hand. "You're aware, aren't

you? You know I just kissed you. Great. Now I really feel like an idiot. You know Sleeping Beauty, right? Probably not. *Hell.* She was awakened with a kiss. I thought it might work, though heaven knows I'm no Prince Charming."

He was only digging himself deeper. "Right. Anyway…" Releasing her hand, he stood and surveyed the surrounding area, looking for anything else that might come after them. Those trimors were going to give him nightmares.

Comfortable that there was no imminent danger of the corporeal kind, he knelt once more beside Tarrys and took her hand again. Still warm, thank God.

"Are you in pain?"

As he stared into her eyes, he felt sure the answer was no. She wasn't in pain. Her eyes, for all that they weren't moving, were amazingly expressive.

"Will you recover?" Again, he thought the answer was yes. "Good. I'll wait for you." Now, he clearly saw distress. "What? You think I'm leaving you like this? Not a chance."

He stretched out his legs and got comfortable, a sound of relief escaping his throat. It felt good to be off his feet.

"You know, eaglet, if it turns out you're really dead and I just *think* I see emotions in your eyes, I'm going to feel like a real fool." But watching her eyes, he grinned. "Except now you're laughing at me."

He lay down beside her, watching a pair of the green-and-white-striped snakes fly across the golden dome as he pulled her slender hand against his chest.

"I'm glad you came, Tarrys. It's a hard thing to admit, but I'd be dead if you hadn't." He squeezed her hand, then rubbed her warm, soft skin with his thumb. "Sorry for pushing so hard. I thought you'd give up, but you've got the stamina of a marathon runner. Now I realize sending you away was the last thing I should have been doing. I hate Harrison's being right even more than I hate being wrong."

He rolled onto his elbow where he could see her eyes. "I do need your help."

She blinked.

The realization jerked Charlie upright. "It's wearing off."

Her hand convulsed in his and he rubbed it as if improving her circulation would somehow make the poison wear off faster. Finally, she gasped in a deep, desperate breath of air, then coughed it out. The mottling, he noticed, was gone.

Charlie helped her sit up, bracing her with an arm around her slim shoulders as the coughing fit slowly subsided.

"I'm glad you warned me about the paralysis or I might have had you buried by now."

Tarrys looked up at him, her violet eyes shuttering her emotions as they hadn't when she was paralyzed. "You shouldn't have waited with me."

"Didn't you hear me when I was talking to you?" He'd already had his half of this discussion.

"Yes, but you don't understand. I can't keep up with you."

"You're still here, aren't you?"

"Barely. You don't know what it's been costing me to keep going. Even when I shot the trimors I was dizzy with exhaustion. I can't keep up with your pace, Charlie."

"I'll slow down."

"No." Her expression turned earnest as she leaned forward. It was all he could do not to meet her halfway and taste those lips again. Lips that were now free to kiss him back.

"I came to help you, not hold you back," she said. "You have to reach the princess. Your world is depending on you."

"Tarrys..." He settled his hand on her jaw and rubbed his thumb over her cheek. "I can't keep up that pace, either. I was being an ass. I thought if I pushed you hard enough, you'd beg off and tell me you had someplace else to go."

"I don't."

"I know." He took her hands and rubbed his thumbs over the soft skin of their backs, the friction going through him like electricity. His gut reaction was to pull her closer, but he felt a tension in her. A resistance. So he held her hands and met her gaze. *Fell* into her gaze. Why had he never noticed that her eyes were deep as the ocean, bottomless wells of violet? Why did she have this pull on him?

He dropped his gaze slightly, breaking the connection as he focused instead on her mouth. And totally forgot what he'd meant to say. That lower lip fascinated him. Just slightly too big in a way that sent shafts of heat firing through his body. All he wanted to do was taste it again.

But she was looking at him with misery in her eyes. His mind gave him a kick. *She wasn't fast enough.* That's what he'd meant to respond to.

He met her gaze. "You're more than fast enough, Tarrys. What's more, you're tough. I admit I didn't think you would be." He gave her a self-deprecating grimace. "You don't exactly look the part. But you're a hell of a warrior. If you'd panicked when you saw those cats, we'd both be dead." He shook his head. "You were amazing."

He'd never spoken truer words. Not only had she kept going when, by her own admission, she'd been close to collapse. But she'd done what she must to save them, and trusted him to do the same.

She watched him uncertainly as if she wanted to believe his words and wasn't quite sure she could.

Squeezing her hands, he released her. "Let's pick up the arrows, get some water, then find a sheltered spot to take a break. We could both use a nap."

They rose as one, then turned in opposite directions to search for the arrows. But his gaze kept going back to her, admiration rising inside him. He recognized in her that same rare strength he'd had to find in himself during SEAL training, the most physically grueling training in the U.S. military. To make it through, he'd had to learn to isolate the pain and discomfort and ignore them, a feat that had demanded a strength of will and spirit few people possessed.

Yet in this delicate-looking little female, he'd found both.

The realization humbled him. He'd long ago figured out that size had nothing to do with that kind of strength. Many of the best SEALs weren't physically imposing men. But never would he have expected to find such toughness in such a small woman. Was it her race? Was this what the Marceils were all about?

Or was he simply beginning to understand Tarrys? Was he starting to see in her that same drive to win, no matter the circumstances, no matter the odds, that was in him? The reason he'd become a SEAL in the first place.

They'd make a good team. As he bent to pluck an arrow from the grass beside the stream, an odd sense of calm settled over him. Accepting her as his partner somehow soothed the ragged sense of chaos that had ridden him since he'd arrived in this place. He was a highly trained, skilled warrior used to being thrown into situations that were out of his control. But always with a team. Never alone. And the situations had been based in a world he understood. A world where the grass and flowers grew where they were planted and invisible animals didn't attack from thin air. His skills had been honed in *that* world, not this.

Esria was unlike any place he'd ever imagined. Alone, he'd be lost. With Tarrys at his side, he might just stand a chance. Assuming he could get his growing attraction under control.

Tarrys had risked her freedom to come after him. She threw her heart into everything she did. Everything he knew about her told him the woman didn't do casual. Neither did he when it concerned his missions. But when it came to relationships? He didn't do serious. A combination that could only end badly, especially now that he'd come to the conclusion he needed her bow arm, her knowledge, and her cool head. Now that he was committed to keeping her by his side for at least another month.

He closed his eyes, trying to shut her out of his senses. She was making hash of his brain.

Having her as a partner might help keep him alive, but at what cost? All he could think of was touching her. Kissing her.

Yeah, if he didn't cool it with the lustful thoughts, they were both going to be in trouble. She was already wreaking havoc on his concentration. And if this continued, he was going to wind up hurting her. She didn't deserve that. And he didn't need an armed and skilled warrior wishing him dead.

Tarrys woke and looked around, noting the russet night sky. For a moment, she was disoriented until her gaze caught on Charlie leaning against the tree beside her, lines of exhaustion on his face.

A faint smile warmed his eyes when he saw her. "How are you feeling?"

"Fine." She sat up, rubbing the sleep out of her eyes with her knuckles. "I feel rested."

"Good. I've been practicing with my bow." He gave her a tired grin. "If we're ever attacked by trees, I'm your man. As long as they don't move."

She smiled softly. "You need to sleep."

"I do." He yawned heavily. "I leave it to you to watch for ghost cats or whatever else we need to beware of."

Tarrys nodded. "Sleep well, Charlie Rand."

As he lay down, the flowers spread before him, offering him a bed. He settled onto the blanket of pink and closed his eyes. Almost at once, his breathing turned deep and even.

She watched him for long minutes, taking advantage of the opportunity to drink her fill as her gaze roamed the strong bone structure of his face, admiring the way his expression softened in sleep. Her heart beat a quick, strong rhythm as pleasure and warmth thrummed through her blood. Yes, he was beautiful to look at, but he was equally beautiful on the inside. A strong man, yet a good man.

And he'd absolutely stolen her heart.

Forcing her gaze from the man lying beside her, she scanned the small woods that concealed them for any sign of movement. Since trimors rarely attacked at night, her bigger concern was that they might be caught by a wandering Esri.

She stretched her limbs, anxious to get moving again now that she was rested, but Charlie needed the same chance to sleep that he'd afforded her. He'd felt guilty, she knew, for pushing her so hard and had insisted they stop the moment they'd found a patch of woods thick enough to conceal them.

It was odd to have someone worry about her. Nice, in a way, but uncomfortable, too, because she feared that his guilty feelings and concern for her could cause him to do things that weren't in his own best interest. Or the interest of his world.

He was a man who protected others, putting their needs before his own. Only such a man would have undertaken this journey in the first place, selflessly risking his life to try to save his world.

She was here to help him succeed in that

mission, not to cause him to fail out of his misguided belief that he now needed to protect her.

Something moved in her chest, something warm and full, as she remembered the look in his eyes as he'd bent over her, the worry creasing his forehead, as she'd lain immobile. He should have left her there and continued on. Instead he'd watched over her.

He'd kissed her. Her very first kiss.

She smiled, quickly, fleetingly, wishing she'd been able to feel it. He'd said he was only trying to break the poison's spell, but she'd seen something in his eyes as he'd held her hands afterward. She'd felt something in his gaze. Something warm with a sharpness that hinted at lust.

A part of her delighted at the thought that he might desire her in that way. But a bigger part of her didn't want that from him, that physical intimacy that mimicked true caring but wasn't.

And if Charlie Rand decided he wished to

mate with her? As much as she might wish to be her own master, she feared she'd never find the strength to deny him.

Chapter 5

Something was wrong with him.

Ever since he woke hours ago, Charlie had felt achy and tired. And god-awful thirsty. How many times had he stopped to drink from the stream they were following into the foothills of the mountains? Too many times to count, yet the sweet, clear water never seemed to assuage his thirst. Wouldn't it be a bitch if he was coming down with a virus? Here, of all places. He'd brought a first-aid kit with the basics, but if he came down with the flu, he'd just have to take a couple of Tylenol and tough it out. He didn't have time to be sick.

Tarrys walked beside him, no longer having to run to keep up. Beside the stream, on the slope high above, a herd of small red polka-dotted deer drank from the stream. As a pair of flying snakes dive-bombed them, they darted off.

Tarrys made a sound of amusement beside him and he glanced at her curiously.

"The snakes entertain themselves," she explained. "And me." The red and gold highlights in her short brown hair caught the golden glow of the sky, igniting hidden color. Was it his imagination, or had her hair grown overnight? The sleek dark cap was starting to lie down in places instead of sticking up like a crew cut.

"How are you feeling this morning?" he asked her.

"Well, thank you." Her eyes turned fathomless as her mouth quirked up in a soft Mona Lisa smile. Her expression hid a multitude of thoughts.

And he wanted to know every one, he realized. Like her hair, the woman was a maze of hidden depths and secrets he longed to explore. She'd become a puzzle to him, a pretty little puzzle he needed to solve.

"No residual effects from the poison?"

She shook her head. "No. I'm fine."

"Good." He wished he could say the same.

They continued on, following the sloping path in companionable silence. Though Charlie constantly scanned for potential dangers, his senses kept zeroing in on his partner. The woman couldn't be dressed any less attractively, with that now-bloodstained, torn, sacklike gown. No makeup. Less-than-stylish haircut.

He didn't like to think of himself as shallow, but being a fit and relatively decent-looking male, he was used to his choice of women. His tastes generally ran to the stylish professional types in their trim suits, high heels and expensive haircuts.

Maybe that's why he'd never really noticed Tarrys before with her bald head and shapeless Redskins sweatshirts. On the roof, yesterday, he'd seen a different woman. He'd seen her *as* a woman. And now he couldn't seem to forget.

Charlie opened his mouth to make small talk, just to hear her voice, but every question he wanted to ask her seemed wrong. *So, what was life like with Baleris? Do you miss being a slave?*

Jesus.

"What's beyond the dome?" he asked instead, glancing skyward.

She cut him a look that was almost amused, as if she'd been listening to his thoughts. "What's beyond *your* sky?" she countered.

"Space. Other stars."

Her eyes turned thoughtful. "I don't know. No one studies our world like you do yours."

"Scientists would have a field day with this place."

If they survived it. The thought was in her eyes, and in his own head. Neither voiced it and he struggled to find a subject that would lighten the mood.

"My team back home is full of pranksters."

She threw him a curious look. "What is a prankster?"

"Someone who enjoys playing good-natured tricks and jokes on others."

Tarrys lifted a single brow and he found himself grinning, partly in anticipation of the stories he wanted to tell her and partly because she was here with him, waiting for him to tell them.

"Between ops, we were always pulling pranks on one another." He regaled her with the stories, about pouring packing popcorn through the sunroof of the Commander's Camry on his birthday, and breaking into his buddy's town house to line the stairs with dozens of Dixie cups full of water.

As he talked, the smile on Tarrys's pretty face bloomed, lighting him up inside like a thousand-watt lightbulb. But he had yet to make her laugh. And he really wanted to hear her laugh.

"Okay, here's the best one. My buddy Dunc

is a grade-A practical joker who married a woman just like him last spring."

The eyes Tarrys turned to him shone with anticipation, her mouth already starting to turn up. His breath caught, the slam of desire to kiss her sudden and nearly overwhelming. But he continued, his need to hear her laughter nearly as great as his need to kiss her.

"We decided we had to get them both, and good. So as a welcome home from the honeymoon, the guys and I hid alarm clocks all around their bedroom, each set to go off at a different hour. The first was buried in the hamper." Charlie started chuckling, watching Tarrys's disbelieving smile with delight. At the sound of her giggle, his heart tripped.

"After the third alarm went off, Dunc turned on all the lights and went on a massive alarm clock hunt. The two of them *thought* they'd rooted out the rest. But they missed the one under the bed."

Tarrys's laughter erupted like a song, as clear and beautiful as he'd known it would be. As perfect. As right. A soft yet brilliant light casting out the darkness. Goose bumps broke out on his arms, then were gone, a visceral reaction he couldn't even begin to explain.

Grinning like a fool, he continued the story. "An hour after they finally went back to sleep, that last one went off. Dunc said they both shot up, then started laughing. And started planning their revenge."

Tarrys's musical laughter floated away. "What did they do?" she asked, still grinning.

Charlie's smile turned wry. "I'm going to have to get to know you a little better before I spill that story."

"Tomorrow, maybe?" she asked hopefully.

"Next year, maybe."

Her expression turned wistful. "I'm sorry I didn't get a chance to meet these friends of yours."

"You'll meet them. I'll introduce you when we get back."

She nodded, but the laughter and amusement were gone from her eyes. Instead he saw regret and resignation. The belief that she wouldn't make it back.

A belief he refused to share.

As Tarrys looked out over the blue landscape toward the forest that hemmed them between stream and trees as they walked, she wondered how a human could possess such magic. Charlie's enchantment wove around her, his power over her growing with every minute she remained in his company. Never had she felt so comfortable with another person.

When was the last time she'd laughed so freely? When was the last time she'd laughed at all? In the human realm, perhaps, watching a television comedy. But never with such pleasure, such joy. Charlie made her happier than she'd ever been, yet desperately wary, for she felt herself falling under his spell. A magic from which she feared there would be no escape.

Beside her, Charlie made a sound of disbelief. "What on earth...?"

Her gaze followed his to where a large yellow animal lumbered up the far bank of the stream.

"What is it?" he asked. "It looks like a cross between a crab and a giant sea turtle."

"They're called cralmonts. They're harmless. And not very good eating."

"Speaking of eating…I'm getting hungry." Charlie patted his chest. "We need to preserve the little bit of food I'm carrying for as long as we can. Kade said the fruit here is all edible, but I haven't seen anything that looks like fruit."

Tarrys glanced at him, watching his keen eyes scan the distance. "Did he tell you how to call the fruit from the trees?"

His gaze cut to her, a look in his eyes that was at once doubtful and amused. "He told me some mumbo jumbo, but I think I'd feel like a fool trying it."

She smiled, amazed at how easily her mouth turned up when she looked at him now. He grinned back at her, his gaze dropping to her mouth, setting her pulse to racing as it lingered there.

"You're not in D.C. anymore, Charlie."

"I noticed." A huskiness that hadn't been there moments ago deepened his voice. Slowly, his gaze lifted to hers and in his eyes she again saw that intensity, that desire.

Her heart tripped, her cheeks growing warm, and she turned away. "The land provides. It's said that in the old days, when the seven stones still resided in Esria, the trees were laden with fruit at all times."

"And now they're barren." His voice remained rich and deep with awareness, even as he allowed her to pretend the air hadn't grown thick and charged between them. "So your world *has* missed those stones."

"In some ways, yes. The land still provides when asked, but not otherwise. And not as conveniently. It used to be that all a person had to do was wish for food and a fruit tree appeared. A wish for water created a pond. Now we have to ask, and even then it doesn't often work if there's already a stream or a fruit tree nearby."

"Such a hardship," he drawled.

Tarrys tried to lift an imperious brow as Larsen would have done, but found herself smiling instead. "You don't think walking to the tree is hard?"

The smile that crinkled the corners of his hot eyes charmed her. Pleasure fluttered inside her chest. And something else. Excitement. Anticipation.

"Show me how it works." His low, softly cajoling tone caressed her senses.

She cut her gaze at him. "Why don't you try it first using Kade's directions. I'll critique your efforts."

"Critique my efforts, huh?" Knowing laughter lit his eyes.

She motioned him toward one of the trees at the edge of the wide, dense wood. "Come. Let's test your fruit-calling prowess."

As they crossed the blue ground, Charlie walked closer than he usually did, so close that his arm accidentally bumped hers, and their hands caught and momentarily tangled. She was starting to feel winded, her heartbeat quick and sharp, though she was barely exerting herself.

Together, they approached a large colin tree, its dark blue bark slick as silk, its leaves as orange as the fruit Aunt Myrtle sometimes squeezed for juice at breakfast. Tarrys rested her hand on the bow slung over her shoulder as she turned to Charlie, who was standing so close their hips nearly touched.

"Do it," she urged.

His gaze snagged hers, his eyes burning suddenly with a bright fire. She forgot how to breathe.

"Call the fruit." Her words dissipated into nothing, but she ducked away, putting space between them.

Charlie watched her with those hungry eyes for several more seconds before he turned to the tree, taking a deep, long breath. Finally, he stepped forward and placed his palms against the bark.

He grunted with surprise. "It's soft."

"Yes. Say the words, Charlie."

"I feel like an idiot," he muttered. "Provide, tree."

Tarrys grimaced, then shook her head with a laugh. "You have to say it like you're asking, not as if you're disgusted with the whole thing."

The look he swung her way was half glare, half amusement. With a put-upon sigh, he tried again, his words monotone. "Please, oh mighty tree. Provide me with the fruit my stomach craves."

"You're going to starve, you know."

Charlie stepped back and motioned to the tree with both hands. "Your turn." Though a smile lingered on his mouth, there was an un-easiness in his eyes that told her he was still very uncomfortable with the strangeness of her world. As she'd once been with his.

She stepped past him, placed her own palms against the smooth trunk of the tree, and murmured, "Please, oh Esria, provide." A short distance above her head, two fat colin fruits appeared suddenly.

With a smile, she turned to find Charlie closer than he'd been a moment before, his gaze not on the fruit but on her smile. Her mouth.

Her pulse leaped to her throat, a blend of desire and fear that echoed from all those times the Esri had forced that desire. Like those times, she was helpless to pull away when Charlie lifted his hand and stroked her cheek with infinite gentleness, his thumb sliding over her bottom lip, soft as air.

A desire unlike any she'd ever felt rose inside her, filling her lungs and her chest, sending her heart into a fury.

He must stop. She had to tell him to stop. But she remained rooted, unable to pull away as he lowered his head to kiss her. His mouth touched hers, featherlight and warm, igniting a fire inside her like kindling torched.

With a ragged breath, she pressed her mouth

against his, desperate for more of the glorious feelings that made her breasts ache and sent damp, throbbing heat to pool between her legs.

Charlie groaned, one hand sliding into her hair, the other going around her, pulling her against his hard body as the kiss turned from soft to desperate, from sweet to fierce in a hot instant. His need poured over her, driving her own to heights she'd never imagined. A need all the more powerful because it wasn't wholly physical, but encompassed her spirit, her mind and her heart. Everything inside her longed to immerse herself in this man, to have him immerse himself in her. To get closer to him in every way.

And he clearly felt the same. His hands were suddenly everywhere. Her hair, her back, her buttocks, pressing her against the hard thickness of his arousal.

She slid her arms around his neck, holding on as his tongue moved against her lips. When she opened her mouth in surprise, his tongue slid inside. Shock turned quickly to pleasure at the feel of this strange closeness, at the taste of him and the incredible intimacy. A groan of that same pleasure rose from his throat. Their mouths fused, need whipped her about like a flag in a storm, yanking her out of herself, ripping away the control she'd clung to so hopelessly.

She *needed*. Sweet Esria, she needed him to hold her, to touch her. To enter her. How could the mere touching of mouths send her body into such a spiral of desire? Never had she felt such a thing naturally.

And she'd felt it unnaturally too many times to count. Esri males couldn't mate an unready female without experiencing pain, so they forced that readiness through enchantment— a violent and unnatural desire that never extended beyond that place between her thighs.

Comparing what she was feeling now, in Charlie's arms, to that miserable parody of true passion was like comparing freedom to slavery. This hunger overwhelmed and, unlike that forced upon her by an Esri, wouldn't end with a quick mating, she was sure of it.

If she ever gave herself wholly to Charlie Rand, their mating would only make the hunger worse. For she instinctively knew it would be a hunger that would haunt her and plague her for the rest of her long, long life.

The fear of that misery shook her out of the frenzy of wanting and she wrenched away.

Charlie let her go, though he watched her with eyes that were at once hot and dazed. "Wow. That was…*amazing.*"

Taking deep, calming breaths, willing her heart to quit racing, Tarrys slid away from the tree, putting distance between them before she lost the struggle and returned to his arms.

She didn't want this. Why was he attracted to her? Why couldn't they simply enjoy each other's company without this *hunger?*

"Tarrys."

Tarrys took a deep, shuddering breath and turned, catching the round green colin fruit Charlie tossed to her. She hazarded a quick look at his face, but he'd managed to shutter his expression.

"We'd better get going," he said evenly.

She nodded and fell into step beside him as they walked along the edge of the woods. The comfortable silence they'd traveled in was gone, awareness coloring every move, every look. But she was determined to find a way back to that easy camaraderie.

After a while, she asked him to tell her another story from his life and he complied, falling into an account of some of his college exploits. The tension between them slowly eased then exploded again when a flash of gray darted from the brush, a Marceil male dashing out of the woods not twenty yards ahead.

Tarrys's startled gaze collided with Charlie's.

Moments later, a tall, white Esri emerged from the trees. "Halt, slave!" This Esri wasn't dressed in the uniform of the Royal Guard as Charlie was, but in a tunic of shimmering, faded blue and brown leggings.

As the Marceil pulled up, jerked back by

the command, the Esri's white face swiveled toward them, bright yellow-green eyes fastening on them.

Beside her, Charlie tensed, the warrior readying for battle.

Tarrys began to shake.

Chapter 6

Even from this distance, Charlie could feel the aggression, the fury, pouring off the Esri male. He was tall, maybe over six feet, his body lean but not unsubstantial. His curly hair and skin were both white as chalk, his eyes as cold as the grave.

Charlie's heart rate slowly lowered, his mind turning deadly calm, his blood pumping through his veins in a tight, pounding rhythm as his body readied for battle.

With the stream on one side and the woods on the other, there was no way to avoid the bastard. He grabbed Tarrys's wrist, feeling the way she trembled, and pushed her behind him as he continued forward, his walk hard and aggressive. Caution warred with the primitive need to take down the bastard who terrified Tarrys, even as he suspected it wasn't this man in particular who scared her, but the whole freaking race.

"Charlie, you can't let him touch you." Tarrys's voice carried to him from behind, low and urgent. "If he reaches for you, break his arm, then his neck and every bone in his body. You won't hurt him for more than a few seconds, but you're stronger than he is. He'll back off if you hurt him."

Not a problem, he thought, smiling grimly.

The Esri turned his attention back to his slave. The Marceil stood ramrod straight, his eyes huge with fear as he stared at his master. He was smaller than Tarrys and looked young, no older than a teenager, his lightly tanned head shiny bald.

"You ran," the Esri intoned. "You will administer your own punishment." He flung a knife at the Marceil, hitting him in the face with the handle of the six-inch blade.

The slave merely winced and bent to pick up the weapon that had fallen to the ground. Without pause or hesitation, he rose and stabbed himself through the gut, sinking the blade to the hilt. A scream erupted from his throat, but he merely pulled the bloody blade from his body and stabbed himself again. And again. And again.

"Jesus." Charlie's head swam, his own gut clenching at the horror of what he was witnessing, at the bloodcurdling screams that went on and on and on.

"Don't react," Tarrys whispered at his shoulder. "This is common punishment. He'll heal."

Charlie's jaw clenched until he thought he'd break teeth. His hands fisted until his nails drew blood. Every muscle in his body, every tendon, begged to pummel the Esri bastard until *he* was the one screaming.

But the Esri showed no interest in them. Nor was he standing along the line of their path.

Instead, he showed every indication that he meant to let them pass without incident, giving Charlie no excuse to attack when doing so could prove suicidal.

He wasn't a fool.

But as they drew close, the Esri's gaze shifted to Tarrys. The hair rose on the back of Charlie's neck, a feral sound clawing at his throat. He felt Tarrys move away from the Esri, but he forced himself not to visibly react to her fear. He knew he must treat her as if she really were his slave.

Their path brought them to within a dozen feet of the Marceil who now lay on the blood-soaked ground, still thrusting the knife into his gut, screaming in agony at the self-inflicted torture, unable to stop until his *master* freed him. A common punishment, Tarrys called it. How many times had she been forced to suffer the same?

The thought had his blood boiling, but he struggled to mask his emotion even as the determination to not allow her to become enslaved again set up a pounding beat in his brain and chest.

The Esri continued to stare at Tarrys as they passed, but he never said a word, never engaged either of them in any way.

"Tell me if he starts after us," he told Tarrys softly when they were far enough past that the man wouldn't hear. Looking over his shoulder was a sign of weakness he couldn't afford, but he needed some warning if they were about to be attacked.

"He watches, but does not follow."

"He watches you."

"Yes," she said softly.

"He wants you." The certainty infuriated him.

"He wants another slave and knows I'm not bound to you."

"Like hell you're not bound to me."

"I have hair, Charlie. No enslaved Marceil has hair."

Damn. "So does that mean he knows I'm not Esri?"

"No. You're clearly a dark blood with your human coloring. There aren't many in Esria, but there are some."

"Yet he didn't challenge me for you."

"No. But the next Esri might. Charlie, I hadn't thought my hair would be a problem. It wouldn't be if I'd remained in hiding. But now that we travel together, my having hair will make them wonder if you're too magically weak to enslave me. It's going to put you in danger. I need to scrape it off."

"No." He'd seen the way she touched it, the pleasure her growing hair brought her.

"Then I need to go back to following you, unseen, so if I'm caught they won't suspect your weakness."

"Absolutely not." He glanced over his shoulder at her, frowning. "He's the first Esri we've seen in two days. Once we start into the mountains, we probably won't see another. We should be there by nightfall."

The problem was, Charlie didn't put it past this one to follow them. As they'd drawn close, he'd noticed the cunning look in the Esri's eyes, a look he hadn't liked. A look that had him certain he was going to have to watch his back…and his partner's.

"What's he up to, eaglet?"

"They're returning to the woods. They may have a camp there. Or perhaps a small village. Few people live in the Banished Lands."

When they'd crested the next shallow hill and were safely hidden from prying eyes, Charlie stopped and turned, his gaze searching the horizon even as his arms reached for Tarrys and pulled her tight against him. She came to him willingly, curving her arms around his waist and pressing her forehead to his chest. For long moments, they stood like that, holding each other, letting the joint fear slide away as they drew strength in one another's arms.

"You okay?" he asked quietly.

She looked up at him with a gaze that was at once shy and warm. "I am now."

Sweet. Beautiful. The words flitted through his head as his gaze roamed her face. The need to protect her rose fiercely inside him. But as his gaze fell to her mouth, she dipped her face and pulled away. "We need to keep moving, Charlie, in case he decides to follow."

With a sigh, he let her go, knowing she was right even as longed to kiss her all over again. *Never* had he had a kiss affect him like that last one had. He could still feel the softness of those lips as sweet as wine, could still feel the brand of her body pressed against his, unresisting. The press of her mouth against his had been artless...*innocent.* Every instinct told him she'd never been kissed.

How was it possible she was an innocent?

They fell into step side by side. "I hate the Esri," Tarrys said, her words low and pained.

Any doubt that she'd known the same kind of abuse he'd just witnessed, disappeared. The certainty felt like a kick in the gut. "You've had masters like that, haven't you?"

Her mouth twisted unhappily as she glanced at him with shadowed eyes. "I had Baleris."

Her simple words chilled him. With a sudden

clarity, he understood what she'd risked by coming with him. As he stared at her delicate profile, her sheer courage humbled him.

"You shouldn't have come. You should have stayed in D.C. where you were safe."

Tarrys shrugged. "If you fail, I won't be safe anywhere."

He nodded slowly. She'd said the words before, but he hadn't truly understood. Now he did. If the Esri took over the human realm, how long before she'd be caught and enslaved again?

"Then we're not going to fail."

Slowly, so slowly, her mouth curved into one of her Mona Lisa smiles, her eyes shining with a strength and determination that matched his own. "No. We're not."

He grinned. With a team like this, how could they possibly lose?

But even as the thought went through his head, exhaustion began to pull at him, the unnatural exhaustion of illness. And he wondered if they really stood a chance at all.

* * *

Two days later, they followed the stream out of the foothills and into the mountains. Charlie ran his hand through hair—hair damp with perspiration, though their pace wasn't one that should be making him break a sweat. As much as he tried to deny it, whatever bug he'd been fighting was starting to get the better of him. Each day he'd had to stop more and more frequently and sleep for hours longer than normal. And the thirst was becoming a nearly intolerable and constant companion.

He was still functioning, still moving. But he had to wonder how long until he could no longer do either.

The ever-present breeze stirred the hem of his cloak and rifled cooling fingers through his hair. As they walked, the terrain became increasingly steep, yet the nearby stream rushed no more quickly than it had on flat ground. Gravity appeared to play no part in it.

A movement near the water caught his attention and he watched a fish the size of a small catfish waddle out of the water to nibble on the tall purple grasses that grew along the banks. Large red-and-black butterflies floated on the water.

Charlie's gaze kept moving as it had since he first arrived, cataloguing his environment, looking for danger. Watching for Esri.

And watching Tarrys. As much as he tried to ignore her, his gaze kept returning to the woman at his side. As she walked, her fingers toyed with the soft locks that must have grown an inch since that afternoon three days ago when he'd watched her shoot the bow on her apartment building roof. The magic of this place, he supposed. Now her rich, dark hair was long enough to lie soft against her head and tickle the tips of her ears in a sleek, pleasing cap. His admiring gaze shifted to the play of light on her delicate features. How had he gone months without noticing how pretty she was? Delicate and ethereal. Like a ballerina. She even walked like a dancer, every movement filled with grace and certainty despite the sacklike gown she wore.

But it was that incredible mouth of hers that kept calling to him and to the hunger deep within him.

"Does your hair always grow this fast?"

Tarrys glanced at him from beneath long lashes and dropped her hand to brush at her slave's gown. "I don't know. I haven't had hair since I was a child."

Simple words filled with a sadness he couldn't begin to fathom. When she'd first joined them, he'd assumed Marceils were naturally bald. That's the only way he'd ever seen her.

"Did Baleris make you chop your hair?"

Her fingers were back to playing with the dark locks and he watched as they brushed the curve of one delicate ear.

"My first master did, not Baleris." She dropped her hand self-consciously and met his gaze, those violet eyes sharp, if shuttered. "All Marceils are shorn when they're enslaved."

"And they force you to continue to shave it?" The practice seemed barbaric. Then again, shaving her hair was nothing compared to the self-inflicted stabbing.

"No. The power of the Esri's control slowly causes the remaining hair to fall out." She lifted her brows and pursed her mouth. "I didn't know the hair could grow back. I've never known an unenslaved Marceil."

He studied her. "It's growing fast. A lot faster here then it did in D.C."

"I know." A wistful smile lit her features, making him catch his breath even as it pulled an answering smile from him.

"That pleases you."

She nodded, the pleasure lingering in her eyes, lighting them like amethysts. "Of course."

Such a simple thing, hair. Simple and basically unimportant. Then again, he was a guy. His own hair was little more than a nuisance he had to keep remembering to cut. But she'd had it stolen from her, and he knew that was just the tip of the iceberg of what she'd lost at the hands of the Esri.

He wanted to know, he realized. What she'd lost, what her life had been like when she wasn't being raped or forced to stab herself. Who she was behind the strong will and those fathomless eyes.

"Tell me something," he said. "Anything about you or your past."

She glanced at him, a wariness flickering in her eyes he hadn't seen for a while. He frowned, then realized the problem. He hadn't asked. He'd demanded.

And she'd spent too many years as a slave.

He turned on his best boyish charm. "Please? You don't have to tell me anything, Tarrys. Ever. But I'd like to know more about you."

She averted her face, saying nothing, and he wondered if he'd insulted her. But when she turned back to him moments later, a hint of mischief danced in her eyes, making him grin for real.

"My people often helped the humans in the

days before the gates were sealed. Did you know that?"

"No. You mean the Marceils?"

"Yes. They tried to make up for some of the misery the Esri caused your race. You remember us. I did a little research and discovered you remember us quite well, though in a funny kind of way."

Her eyes were still dancing, her luscious mouth trembling at the corners as if struggling not to smile.

"Did we call you pixies or something?"

Her mouth lost the battle. The smile lit her face from within, warming him in a way no smile before ever had.

"Not pixies. These were the days before the Esri enslaved us. Marceils had hair." She lifted her fingers to the soft tufts on her scalp. "Brown hair like mine." She paused for effect, watching him. "The humans called us brownies."

Charlie's eyebrows shot up. "You're kidding."

She shook her head, pleasure dancing in her

eyes. "We've been immortalized in the human consciousness by little girls. Little Brownie Girl Scouts."

Charlie nodded, a funky chill making him shiver. Just when he thought he was getting used to this stuff being real...

"My niece, Stephie, told me the story. That brownies were believed to visit at night and clean up or finish some task after the family went to bed. If the family suspected they had a brownie visitor, they'd leave food and milk in hopes he...or she...would return."

Her smile turned wistful. "My mother told me the same tale." Her expression sobered. "Harrison's daughter is a Brownie?"

"Yeah." The darkness rolled through him, harsh and painful. "She was. Before Baleris touched her." She was lost to them now, her body functioning, but her mind locked up in a place no one could reach.

God, he hated that Esri. He hated all Esri except Kade and, hopefully, Princess Ilaria. And if they didn't find the princess and convince her to seal the gates before King Rith got his hands on the seven stones of power, life as they knew it would end. King Rith intended to tear down the walls between the worlds and enslave the human race.

This mission of his was perhaps the most critical in the history of humanity. No way in hell was he failing it.

But a few minutes later, his scalp began to crawl. "We're being followed."

Tarrys jerked, her wide eyes meeting his gaze. "How do you know?"

"Instinct. The same way I knew you were following me. It could be another Esri."

"It could be the same Esri."

Charlie shook his head. "It's been two days. I would have felt him before now."

"Perhaps. Or perhaps he has a gift that allows him to track us. Either way, it doesn't really matter."

Which was all too true. With his energy flagging, either way, they were in deep trouble.

Chapter 7

Sweat rolled in twin beads down Tarrys's temples as she followed Charlie up the narrow, rocky path. They'd left the forest behind some time ago, though they continued to follow the stream. The colors of the increasingly rugged terrain changed as they rose in altitude, the stones turning a more vibrant red, as if they'd been dipped in blood and sprinkled with silver. Above, the golden sky slowly turned to rust.

Fear rode her shoulders, a continual and growing weight. Not fear for herself. No, her fear lay centered entirely upon Charlie. Not only were there a hundred dangers awaiting him in this land, but something was very wrong with him and they both knew it.

He tried to tell her he was simply suffering from a virus, that he'd be well soon enough. But she saw his weakness growing hour by hour. And she watched the worry darken his eyes.

What would she do if he became seriously ill? She knew nothing about human sickness and cures, and had no skills as a healer.

Her gaze went to him now, traveling over the wide expanse of his broad shoulders, catching a glimpse of his strong profile. Even exhausted and ill, his keen gaze searched for danger every minute of every hour of every day. He was so strong, so capable. A warrior, through and through. But human bodies were inherently fragile.

The thought of such a man being forced to succumb to illness, to a foe he couldn't fight, made her ache almost as much as the thought of losing him.

And the thought of losing him was nearly more than she could bear.

She loved him. Charlie Rand was a good man, a warrior, through and through, ready to fight to protect others. He would kill, and had killed, but not without reason. She believed that.

War was not the way of Esria. Not the human kind of wars, at least. The last true battle had been fought three hundred years ago when Rith captured the queen, princess Ilaria's mother. He was strong, but, it was rumored, not strong enough to take her fairly. So he'd ordered one of his followers to destroy her with the death curse. Of course, the follower was subsequently killed for having ended another Esri's life, even though he'd been acting under orders. But such was the way of royal successions.

Charlie stopped as they reached a level stretch of path and leaned against one of the red rocks, perspiration damp on his brow, his skin several shades too pale.

He swayed on his feet and Tarrys's heart tripped. She looped her arm around his waist. "You need to rest again."

"I'm okay." But he sank to his knees, making a lie of his words. "No. I'm not. I don't know what's wrong with me." He lay down awkwardly on a sprouting blanket of pink flowers as if he'd lost all his strength. "Half an hour. No more."

Tarrys knelt beside him and pulled the bow and quiver off his back, laying them beside him so he could rest more comfortably. Hesitantly, she laid her hand against his forehead as she'd seen Aunt Myrtle do once. She'd heard that human skin grew hot to the touch when a human sickened, but there was no unnatural heat in Charlie's skin. Her gaze caressed his face, flowing over his light brown eyebrows to his closed eyelids and down to his strong, warrior's mouth. As she watched, his lips parted on a low sound that told her he slept.

She stayed there beside him until his color began to return. Perhaps his body simply needed time to adjust to her world. With a soft stroke to his hair, she rose and retraced their path a short way back, placing herself firmly between Charlie and those who followed them.

Climbing onto a large, flat rock, she sat cross-legged to wait. A half an hour, he'd said. And how was she to know when a half hour had passed? If he was sick, he needed to sleep. She knew that much.

Minutes later, she heard the soft pad of feet behind her and turned. "I thought you'd sleep longer…." Her voice trailed off, her heart shooting to her throat. It wasn't Charlie behind her as she'd thought. *It was the Esri.* The one in the blue tunic who'd watched her so covetously as he'd punished his own slave.

Triumph shone in his cruel eyes.

Tarrys leaped to her feet, her heart pounding in her ears, her mouth dry as sand. How had he gotten past her?

Her gaze shot to the spot on the path above her where Charlie still slept, seemingly untouched. She must keep the Esri from seeing him. But as she whirled to jump down from the ledge, to lead him away, a second Esri appeared below, his pale hair glowing like copper beneath the russet sky, a lust-filled smile on his face and a hard promise in his pink eyes.

Her days of freedom were over.

Chapter 8

Charlie woke to the sound of a scream.

He was on his feet before he was fully awake, his brain scrambling to catch up. One glance at the disappearing flowers beneath his feet did the trick. Esria. Check.

"No!" Tarrys's furious voice was laced with a terror that chilled his blood.

He saw her below, surrounded by two Esri, one of which he recognized all too well. *Dammit.* Tarrys was trying to dodge the bastards' grasping hands, but she was too small, her robe too large and unwieldy to allow her quick movement, despite her agility. As Charlie ran down the path to reach her, the bastard in the blue tunic rushed her and clamped his hand around the back of her neck. Instantly, Tarrys stilled, her face a mask of misery and defeat.

Her captor grinned with satisfaction, his teeth gleaming white as he released her. Tarrys didn't run. Instead, with quick desperate motions, she tossed her bow and quiver on the ground, untied her purple sash, then lifted her gown over her head—the only scrap of clothing she wore—and dropped it. As she stood naked but for the band of holly, which clearly hadn't worked, the Esri reached for the ties of his pants.

Charlie's gut tightened, fury roaring in his ears. The bastard had enslaved her with that touch, probably mentally ordering her to undress and she'd been helpless to disobey.

He would rape her and she'd let him, unable to fight.

Like hell.

Charlie leaped onto the open rock and

launched himself at the son of a bitch, tackling him to the ground. The Esri didn't fight the attack, but the moment they hit the rock, he slapped his palm over Charlie's hand. Pain shot through his body of such a ferocity that his vision went white. *Jesus.*

He struggled to free himself, prying the Esri's hand off his. The moment he could move, he retaliated, plowing his fist through the Esri's pale face three times before he realized the Esri wasn't struggling. Was, in fact, watching him with keen interest.

Warning bells went off in his head, Kade's advice flashing through his mind. *Act the aggressor.* He'd done that in spades, but not in the calm, barbaric manner Kade had recommended—breaking bones. Just by the color of his skin and hair, they knew he had human blood. The key was making sure they didn't know exactly how much.

Charlie got to his feet and backed away from the Esri and that hand of his, then glared at the two men.

"She's mine!" he growled.

The man he'd attacked rose to his feet with an ease that mocked Charlie's attack, his eyes glittering with speculation. "Not anymore. You didn't enslaved her. I have."

"Look at his hand," said the second Esri.

With a sinking certainty, Charlie knew what they were looking at. He could feel the sting of a split knuckle and the dampness of blood running down his finger.

"Human," the first man intoned as a malicious smile crossed his face. "And a Sitheen, at that, or my touch would not have caused him pain, but enchanted him. *Catch him.*"

Hell.

"Charlie, run!" Tarrys cried.

If the men had been human, he could have taken them. But they were immortal. He could knock them down all night and day and they'd just keep popping back up for more. Running was never his favorite course of action, but there were times when retreat was the best option. The only option.

Like now.

He dove for Tarrys, bending low as he grabbed her gown and weapons with one hand and slung her over his shoulder with his other. The Esri shouted, but couldn't move fast enough. Charlie tore back between them, up the path, running for his life. For both their lives.

Adrenaline rushed through his system, lending him strength and speed. He felt good again, strong and rested, even though he was certain he hadn't slept long.

Tarrys squirmed against his shoulder, her bare feet kicking his hipbone, her small fists pummeling his buttocks. His hand gripped her bare thighs tighter against him.

"Settle down, eaglet. I've got you… Umph," he groaned as she kneed him in the chest.

"I can't stop! I can't control it." Her warm, round hip pressed against his cheek, filling his nostrils with the intoxicating scent of woman. "When he touched me, he claimed me as his slave. His mark calls me to him, now, and will always do so. My body is trying to get back to him."

Charlie heard her words, his logical mind longing to deny that any such thing was possible, but he knew too well how completely Tarrys could be controlled. And, *dammit,* that was the *last* thing they needed. A yell of frustration lodged in his throat. If he set her down, she'd run straight into the arms of the enemy. As he ran, his legs eating up the path with hard, fast strides, a dismal thought occurred to him.

"Can I trust what you say or does he control your words, too?"

"He can't control my mind like he can a human's. A true human's. And he can only control my speech if he thinks to do it. He didn't this time. His only thought was for my body."

At her words, a vision of her standing naked flashed in his mind—her perfect form, her breasts high and full, her waist slender, her hips gently flared. Even her legs had appeared long and shapely simply because she was so perfectly proportioned, as if he'd specially ordered a leggy brunette, size small.

"Are they following?" he asked.

"Yes. But your speed is faster."

But for how long? Especially with a squirming woman on his shoulder. Hell, they knew he was human. All they had to do was follow him, secure in the knowledge he'd eventually wear himself out. And if he didn't wear himself out, Tarrys would do it for him. Controlled by the Esri, she'd be fighting him every step of the way. He'd always liked a challenge, but enough was enough, dammit.

Tarrys's struggles continued, though her movements, the way she was rocking her hips against his shoulder, felt less like struggling and more like…

The scent of her arousal filled his nostrils, hardening him on the spot.

"Eaglet." As if he didn't have enough distractions without adding a raging hard-on to the list.

"I can't help it." Her voice sounded on the

verge of tears. "Through his touch, he ordered me naked and ready for his penetration. My body is desperate for his mating."

Hell. "How long does it last?"

"Until he's finished with me."

"He's not going to finish," he growled.

Charlie ran full bore up the steep, rocky ridge, his mind whirring, searching for options. The problem was, he didn't dare kill them. Because the moment he did, he'd acquire an Esrian death mark which was apparently the equivalent of a homing beacon. According to Kade, all Esri would not only know immediately what he'd done and to whom, but they'd know where he was. At all times. And feel duty bound to come after him and end his life, thank you very much.

So, no, killing these douche bags wasn't exactly at the top of his list of smart moves at the moment. The problem was, that list was looking damned empty.

The only thing he knew for sure was that he

had to keep ahead of the Esri chasing them. Beyond that was anyone's guess.

Less than a mile later, exhaustion started to nip at his heels. Discomfort had turned to pain a while back, but he'd long ago learned to ignore the pair of them. His body was strong. He knew what it was capable of.

At least he knew what it was capable of in his own world. Never before had he hit such a wall of exhaustion that he'd literally been unable to move another step. Even sick as a dog. Yet he'd done just that earlier today, which told him this was no ordinary illness. It must have something to do with this place.

If he hit that wall, now, with two Esri hot on their heels...

Real fear twisted in his gut. If his body turned traitor on him again, it was all over, for both of them. Unfortunately, that scenario was all too likely.

"Tarrys...I need some alternatives. Anything. I can't outrun them forever."

Her desperate rocking stopped, like a moment's hush in the middle of a windstorm. An unnatural stillness.

Her body went tense as a bowstring. "Charlie...you must release me." The frenzied movements resumed on a deep shudder. "You must let me go back to them."

"No."

"It's the only way. You'll tire too quickly carrying me like this. And I'll be able to stall them."

"Right. While they rape you."

"It won't be rape...not like you think of it. He's made me *need* his penetration. He'll ease my suffering."

"I'm not letting you go." She was his partner now. And no SEAL left his partner behind. Period.

Besides, *sweet Jesus,* he couldn't let them have her.

But minute by minute, her slight weight grew heavier. He was running out of time.

Chapter 9

"Charlie! I know this place." The thread of excitement in Tarrys's voice had Charlie's hopes leaping. "There's an abandoned crystal mine not far from here. The crystals are known to interfere with magic and may help hide us, at least for a little while."

"Thank God." Maybe, *maybe,* they finally had a chance. How many times had a chance been all he'd needed to turn certain defeat into triumph? Though heaven knew how he was going to manage it this time.

"Which way?"

"I don't know. I can't see...."

He swung her off his shoulder, holding her struggling body tight even as her gaze fastened on the path before them. "Up the hill. In the crags ahead, where the bushes grow thick, is the entrance to one of the old mines."

Charlie started forward, dragging her up the rocky path.

"There. Go left," she ordered when they reached the bushes. "Up there. Climb onto the rocks."

He followed her every command.

"Now go left again. I think…" The rock face broke to the right, revealing a small cave no more than five feet high and about the same distance wide.

Bingo.

He pulled her off his shoulder. "Can you put on your dress?" His hands were already full with one hand clamped around her arm and the other holding her gown and weapons.

"Yes, but don't give me the bow. I might try to shoot you."

"Thanks for the warning." He slung the bow

and quiver over his shoulder, then handed her the dress.

Tarrys fought her way into the gown, then he pushed her into the black maw of the low cave and bent low to follow her in. The moment they stepped inside, a red glow lit the small tunnel, revealing a remarkable passage of solid crystal.

Charlie stared around him at the amazing sight, the red glow reflecting everywhere like a million flames. The faint smell of sweet wine reached his nose. "How did it light?"

"The crystal reacts to heat." Her voice was tight, pained. "My bare feet light our way. The touch of your hand would do the same."

"The light is going to give us away."

"No. Not if we're far enough ahead. The light will die behind us, erasing our path."

"Good. Does it burn?"

"The crystal is cool." But the eyes she turned to him were feverish with need, sending another torrent of fire rushing through his body. "The burn comes from inside."

Charlie lowered himself to his knees and

reached out to touch the roughly cut crystal with an unsteady hand. Purple-blue overlaid the red, adding the smell of flowers in a spring rain. Incredible. "The crystals have a smell."

"Yes. Each color smells a little different."

"Let's get out of the mouth. Does it open up inside, or am I going to have to crawl the whole way?" The cold stone was smooth, but hard beneath his knees. No flower bed cushions in here.

"It opens up a little, enough that I'll be able to walk upright. But not enough for you. The Esri never liked these caves because of that. The Marceils are smaller and better suited."

"How far in can we go?"

"Miles and miles, if we need to. I was a child the last time I was here, but I think the mines go all the way through the mountain."

Even better news. If the crystals could hide them, they might just stand a chance of getting away. He started crawling, glad the floor was smooth, at least, if cold.

"Going through the mountain isn't an option

unless there's food stashed in here somewhere," he murmured. "And underwater springs. It'll take at least a week to travel through a mountain this size. Maybe longer."

"The land provides, Charlie. Even within the mountain. But I think there are other ways out. Caves near here. I only ever left the mines once. But we always had water."

"You traveled through these mines as a child?"

"No. I was born here." On the last, her voice tightened, as if the sexual need rose and fell in waves just as her struggles seemed to do.

He stopped talking and concentrated on navigating the strange passage behind her. A high-pitched chirping echoed from deep in the tunnel.

"Sounds like a cricket."

Tarrys gave a shudder. "Mine crickets."

He looked at her sharply. "Are they dangerous?"

"No. They're bigger then the crickets in your world, but no more harmful. One got caught in my hair when I was a girl. I've hated them ever since."

Tarrys remained on her feet, bending low, until the ceiling lifted enough for her to walk upright. Charlie rose to his feet, though he had to bend low to keep from hitting his head on the low, jagged ceiling. He was going to have one heck of a backache by the time he got out of here.

Every now and then, his hand came in contact with the cool smoothness of the crystal wall, adding more light. Each time, the crystal reacted differently to his touch, sometimes glowing bright blue, sometimes bluegreen, sometimes almost purple. The mine snaked and curved, breaking off into more forks than a tree branch. At each fork in the path, Tarrys chose without hesitation as if she knew exactly where she was going. He hoped to God she did. If he had to lead, they'd wind up hopelessly lost.

As Tarrys had predicted, the light illuminating their path disappeared quickly, leaving no trail unless their pursuers were close enough to see it. The Esri weren't likely to find them. Not unless they had a magical way to track them. And that was something he'd rather not think about.

They continued in silence, careful to touch the walls as little as possible. Charlie glanced back over and over, looking for the sign of a light in the distance that would warn him that they were being followed. But the cave remained dark behind them. Slowly, he began to believe they might actually get away.

No sooner had the thought sprouted in his head than Tarrys turned abruptly and launched herself past him.

Charlie's arm shot out to snare her, but the illness was making him slow and his center of balance was off from having to bend over. He caught her at the last possible second, and they went down hard on the crystal.

"He calls me." Tarrys's voice pleaded with him to help her though she fought him like a banshee. One kick of her heel landed

squarely on his jaw sending pain crackling through his head.

He yanked her hard until she was under him, her flailing fists caught in his hands as he pinned her to the floor with his body. Grasping both her wrists with one hand, he fished beneath his tunic for the length of rope he'd brought. Beneath him, her hips rocked feverishly. *Sweet heaven.*

He stared down into her face as she bucked and thrashed, her expression filled with a misery that tore at his heart. Tears leaked from her eyes.

"Charlie, I need…I *need*."

The heat coming from her body burned him inside and out. "How long is this going to last?"

"Until I'm penetrated."

Penetrated. The blood surged to his groin so fast his head swam. It would be so easy. So easy…

"Can you…make yourself come?"

"No. It's not enough. I would have you."

The breath hissed out of his lungs.

"Please, Charlie. Mate with me. *End this.*"

Holy hell.

His baser nature rose to the fore, slapping him on the back. *She needs it, man. It's for her.*

But that was the thing. She didn't want any of this. Her body begged for release to relieve the torture the Esri had inflicted upon her, but that was all. And not nearly enough.

When all was said and done, he refused to help that bastard rape her, even if he longed to lift the hem of her gown and sink himself deep inside her so badly that he was shaking from the need.

"Tarrys…"

Her head thrashed back and forth, tears flowing freely from her eyes. "You don't understand. This won't stop until I have something inside me." She was frantic now, her body shaking, her movements jerky and desperate. *"I must end this."*

He had to find a way to help her. The last thing he wanted was to make this any harder on her than it already was. With his free hand, he gripped her chin, stilling her thrashing head, and kissed her hard.

She met his kiss with a ferocity that left him reeling…and sent his lust spiraling out of control. Releasing her wrists, he shoved his fingers into her short hair, loving the softness, and the feel of her delicate head in his hands. Her arms surged around his neck, pulling him tighter as her frantic tongue met his, as her hips rocked feverishly against his. He kissed her with all the passion that swirled inside him, telling her of his desire while his hand slowly slid down her body.

He moved off her, keeping her penned with one leg as he pulled her gown up and pushed his hand between her damp thighs. Instantly, she struggled against the weight of his leg, trying to spread her own. As he continued to kiss her, inhaling her sweet scent, worshipping her with his mouth, he stroked her wet folds with two fingers, then pushed them deep inside her.

Her cry filled his mouth as she shoved her hips upward, silently screaming for more.

He pushed a third finger inside and she took them all, thrusting against his hand, drenching him in her passion, sweeping him up until his own body shook, desperate for release, damning him for the morals that refused to let him take her.

He ground his mouth against hers as her fingers dug into his hair and she grabbed his head, forcing him closer.

Her hips rose and fell, undulating with the thrusts of his fingers. Her movements grew more frantic, more frenzied. Her groans harsher, needier, and he hoped she was racing toward completion, prayed he wasn't making things worse. The fragrance of her sex changed subtly, floral scents filling the small space until he could almost imagine he was in the middle of a flower garden. The smells burrowed into his pores, twisting his hunger until he thought he would die from the need to fill her.

With a sudden moan, her hands clamped hard

against his head and she filled his ears with the sounds of impending release. Her orgasm hit, washing over him like a warm wind that touched every inch of his flesh, nearly driving him to release. She wrenched her mouth from his, threw her head back, and screamed with passion and relief as he buried his face in her neck, absorbing the feel of her inner muscles contracting hard around his fingers.

He was gasping, panting from reaction to one of the most amazing, most *intense,* sexual encounters of his life. And he hadn't even come.

Slowly her body unbowed. Reluctantly, he pulled his fingers out of her depths and lifted his head from her neck. But as his cheek slid against hers, he felt the dampness of tears.

"Are you okay?" He wished he could see her face, but the crystal lights had gone out and they now lay in perfect darkness.

"Yes." But the crack of her voice and the subtle shaking of her body told him other-wise. She unhooked her arms from around his neck and turned away from him as much as she could with his leg still pinning her to the ground.

His heart contracted. "Tarrys." He felt helpless. She wanted to get away from him, away from what had just happened, but he knew instinctively that if he let her curl into herself, he wouldn't know how to get her back.

So he eased off her and pulled her against him, her back to his chest, his arm hooked around her waist, pulling her tight.

"Tarrys, I know he controlled you. I know he did this to you." But his words had no effect. Her body remained taut and shaking, and he knew she had to be crying.

She'd begged him to enter her. *Begged* him. And he'd refused.

Was that part of the problem? Did she think he hadn't wanted her?

"Tarrys...I wanted to come inside you so badly I thought I was going to die from it. But when I make love to you, it's going to be because *we* decide to. You and me together.

Not because a son of a bitch Esri forced the need on you."

Charlie felt her soften ever so slightly and suspected he'd hit the source of her pain. His rejection had hurt her. Humiliated her. And that's the last thing he'd meant to do.

He lifted his head and kissed her damp cheek. "Taking you would have been like helping him rape you. I couldn't do that to you. I *wouldn't* do that to you. You're my partner. I would never do anything to risk hurting you like that."

Though she didn't respond, her shaking slowly subsided. When she moved as if to roll onto her back, he released his tight hold on her, then rose onto his elbow, propping his head on his hand.

The move lit one of the crystals and he found her wiping the tears off her face to look up at him with pained, troubled eyes. "I don't want you to mate with me...to make love to me," she said miserably.

Not exactly the words he'd longed to hear,

especially considering he was hard as a rock for her and suspected he was likely to stay that way. But he wasn't surprised, not after all the abuse she'd taken. And he was suddenly, profoundly glad he *hadn't* taken advantage of her.

He released her waist and lifted his hand to stroke her cheek with his thumb. "I'm attracted to you, Tarrys. I can't help it. And I probably can't stop it." He cupped her face, forcing her to look at him, to see the truth in his eyes. "But I'll never do anything you don't want me to. Ever. I promise you."

Her chin trembled and her mouth compressed with a misery that broke his heart. Tears rolled from her eyes. But she nodded and he leaned forward to lay a soft kiss on her temple.

"Rest. I'll keep watch."

Without saying anything, she turned and scooted back against him, gifting him with her trust. Charlie pulled her tight, relief washing through him, a warmth growing deep in his chest.

He'd die before he let anyone hurt her again.

But a short time later, that terrible exhaustion slammed him like a wall of bricks.

"Tarrys…I've got to sleep. I've got to tie you first, so he can't…" Struggling against a thick, body-numbing lethargy, he managed to retrieve his rope from his gear vest. With slow, awkward movements, he tied her wrists together, looping the rope around himself to tie it at the back of his waist. She wouldn't free herself. But if the Esri found them while he slept, all his promises to keep her safe were forfeit.

Chapter 10

Tarrys lay in total darkness beneath the warm weight of Charlie's arm, listening to the mine crickets and watching for sign of light in the distance. A sign that the Esri had followed them into the mines. Charlie slept behind her, his deep, even breaths stirring her hair, his body warm and solid. But the feeling of being cherished was an illusion. And the warmth wouldn't penetrate the chill of her heart.

Charlie Rand would never again mistake her for anything but what she was…a slave and a tool of the Esri.

For a few precious days, she'd seen respect

in his eyes. Friendliness. Even genuine desire. Charlie had looked at her as if she were a woman. A human woman, not the little oddity he'd seen her as at first.

For a few precious days, she'd felt strong and whole, as if she could be the partner he called her. She'd felt she could be worthy of him. As a friend. Perhaps, someday, a lover. Even donning her slave's garb again to follow him into Esria had been an act of strength, because she'd donned it of her own free will. She'd chosen to follow him despite his wishes. There was power in that.

But that power had been stripped away with the touch of an Esri hand.

Charlie had seen the truth. He'd seen what she was—nothing but a slave used for men's basest desires. Powerless. Useless to him as guide or friend now that she was controlled by his enemy.

She'd never felt so worthless or desolate in her life.

Tears burned her eyes as she realized it was

only a matter of time before her new master claimed her. Never again would she be free.

She shifted her bound hands, covering Charlie's much larger one, needing the feel of her skin on his as he held her tight. The tears ran faster as she clung to him, knowing this warmth and kindness might well be her last.

If Charlie wished to survive, he needed to let her go.

That she was still with him was a testament to the deep vein of loyalty that drove this man. Loyalty that would get him killed if her new master had the power to control her from afar. He could, conceivably, use her as a weapon against Charlie. The best thing would be for her to go back to them.

But Charlie would never allow that. And if she managed to get herself free? He'd only come after her again, and almost certainly get himself killed this time.

Her fingers curved around the edge of his hand. She knew he needed to let her go. And desperately hoped he wouldn't.

Something caught her eye—a tiny flicker of blue light against the mat of black. Her pulse jumped.

"Charlie." Her hand gripped his tightly. "Charlie, wake up. You have to get moving."

She felt the change in him though he made no movement, no sound to indicate he was awake.

"I see light," she whispered. "The Esri have followed us into the mines."

"Damn." The softly spoken word barely reached her ear, but he started to move.

Tarrys dug her fingers into his hand. "Be careful. If I can see their light, they'll be able to see ours. Light your way by pressing a single fingertip against the crystal. They should be too far away to see it."

"Your bare feet light the crystal with every step. We've got to wrap them first."

"You must leave me here, Charlie. You must go on without me."

"No." His arms tightened around her once, before releasing her. A tiny circle of blue light ignited on the floor at her head and in that tiny glow she saw the hard planes of his face as he rose.

"Charlie, they aren't following us. They're following me. The bond this Esri has with me must be strong for him to be able to track me despite the crystals. Without me, you stand a chance. With me, none at all."

"I'm not giving you to them." He knelt beside her and pulled out his knife. "This gown's going to get a little shorter. I hope you don't mind."

"Charlie…" She sighed, wanting to fight him yet, just as desperately, wanting him to over-rule her. She didn't want to leave him. "Charlie, they already own me. They could use me to hurt you. You must save yourself."

He continued with what he was doing as if she hadn't spoken. As thoroughly and gently as he did everything, he cut two strips from the hem of her gown and tied them around her feet.

"I need you," he said, loosening the ropes binding her hands. "I don't know my way through here."

"Neither do I."

"You've done damn well so far."

"I knew how to get in, but I haven't been here since I was a child. All I know is that at some point the mine tunnels open into large caverns that extend through the center of the mountain. I believe there are other ways out on this side, but I don't know where they are."

Charlie reached around her waist, tying the rope like a belt.

"I can't be your guide, Charlie, only your companion, and now that I'm enslaved, I can't be even that. I'll be your death."

He didn't seem to be listening. "Sorry about the leash, but I don't want you getting away from me if he calls you again." As he glanced at the floor, his brows drew together. "What did I do with my bow and quiver?"

"I took them off you when you fell asleep on the path."

Charlie groaned. "And I never picked them up again. I heard you scream and never looked back. At least we've got yours. Let's go." He gave a small tug on the rope, rose to a hunch, and lit another small dot of light. "You go first. If you've been here before, your subconscious probably remembers more than you think it does."

"Charlie…" She tried to stop the forward movement, desperate to make him understand, but he just gave her an amused look and a small push. She glared at him. "You're going to get yourself killed over an inappropriate sense of loyalty. I'm a slave. I've never been more than that. I can never be. It's my fate. It's my purpose."

"It's nobody's purpose to be used and abused by another. You're too smart to believe that."

"You're not hearing a word I say."

She felt a tug on the rope, stopping her, felt his hands cup her shoulders as he pulled her back against him.

"I've heard *every* word you've said. I just don't happen to agree with them. We're going to get through this together. I'm not letting you go back to that. *Ever.*"

His words, velvet-coated steel, filled her with as much fear as relief. He was endangering himself. But, oh, how she loved him for it. She lifted her hand and pressed it against his cheek. "Then we can't fail. I can't watch you die."

"We're not going to fail." She felt his lips against her temple then a gentle push with his hands. "Now quit arguing with me and get moving, woman."

The gentle affection in his words warmed her, nearly tugging a smile from her despite the direness of their situation. Inside, her heart filled, expanding with a pressure that was almost painful as she fell in love more deeply than she'd ever thought possible. Charlie Rand was strength and courage, kindness and tenderness. And by far the finest man she would ever know.

For a moment, she pulled his protectiveness around her like a soft fleece blanket and tried to believe that he could really get them out of Esria. But the fear in her heart wouldn't be appeased.

* * *

"There's been no sign of the Esri for more than an hour," Charlie said, miles later. "Do you think we could have lost them? Could the bond be weakened through distance like this?"

Tarrys glanced over her shoulder at the top of Charlie's bent head as he walked, hunched over beneath the low ceilings. "I think they're taking breaks. They're probably hating these low ceilings as much as you are, but the Esri have little tolerance for discomfort."

"I hope they take a long…break…this time. I've got to…"

Tarrys whirled, catching him around the waist as he slammed into the wall, lighting the space bright red, releasing the faint scent of fermenting fruit.

"Tired," he said. His knees buckled and she managed to get him onto the floor without banging his head. By the time she laid him out, he was already asleep.

Fear hammered in her chest as she brushed his cheek with her fingers. Something was very wrong with him. She knew just enough about human illness to know he needed help. And she had no idea how to offer it.

He looked tired. Unwell. He looked...

A chill traveled over her skin as she caught the sight of something on his neck. A greenish marking. She reached for him and pulled back the edge of his tunic.

Mottling. The green mottling of trimor poisoning.

Chapter 11

Charlie blinked, waking slowly to the sight of a tiny red night-light. No, he realized. Not a night-light. A glowing spot of crystal wall, illuminating Tarrys. She sat beside him, her arms wrapped around her up-drawn knees, her chin on her arms as she watched him with worry-filled eyes.

Charlie pushed himself up until he sat beside her. "What happened?" He vaguely remembered feeling tired. Tired, hell. More like someone had hit him over the head with a baseball bat.

"You fell asleep," Tarrys said softly. If anything, her brows drew closer together.

Glancing down the dark tunnel, he searched for distant light. "Any sign of the Esri?"

"No. Charlie, I know why you've been feeling the way you have."

"I have a virus." A big, honking Esrian virus, if he had to guess. He'd never had anything ambush him in quite this way, with so little warning. He could barely trust his own body anymore.

Which was kind of ironic, given Tarrys's situation. He frowned, suddenly remembering he'd collapsed so fast he hadn't had time to think about securing her, let alone doing it. The end of her rope, the end he'd been holding in his hand, was now tied around his wrist.

He held up his hand. "You did this?"

"Yes. I'd hoped it might wake you up if I was forced to try to go to him."

Clearly, thankfully, the bastard hadn't called her. Charlie rose, bending at the waist to keep from clobbering his head on the low ceiling. "Let's get going."

"Charlie, we need to talk."

"We'll talk while we travel."

Tarrys rose with an easy, fluid grace before he could even offer her a hand, and he ushered her in front of him, envying her height. The ceilings through here were several inches above her head, leaving her free to walk upright. "I'm kind of surprised you're still here," he told her. "The way you were wanting me to let you go."

"I only wanted to leave to help you. Now I have to stay to do that." The passage was wide enough for the two of them to walk side by side and she fell into step beside him.

"What do you mean?" The grave expression on her face didn't bode well.

"You were poisoned, Charlie. By the trimor."

He frowned. "It didn't attack me."

"It must have broken your skin with its horn."

He reached for his shoulder, rubbing it. "I felt his horn snag on my tunic for just an instant, but I swear he didn't break through."

But her expression made it clear she didn't believe him.

Charlie scowled. "Do I look paralyzed? I promise you, it's just a virus."

Without answering, she looked away, and they continued on in silence for several minutes before she spoke again.

"Do you remember the way my skin looked after the trimor attacked?" She turned back, her eyes sharp and demanding. "That green mottling? As you fell asleep, I saw the same green pattern on your neck."

Charlie looked at his hands, turning them over. Nothing.

"It went away quickly," she said. "But I know what I saw."

"Then why aren't I paralyzed?"

She looked to the ceiling with a shake of her head. "I don't know. You're human. And you probably only got a tiny amount of the poison. But this has to be why you keep tiring. Your body's trying to fight it."

Charlie's jaw clamped tight. At least he knew why he'd turned into the walking dead.

"Is there an antidote?" He reached for his

canteen, so damned thirsty. Was the poison to blame for that, too? He offered her a drink, but she shook her head.

"There is an antidote. The root of the carnasserie bush. But we have to get out of the mines to find it."

Charlie took a long pull of water, forcing himself to stop long before his thirst was quenched. "Then we have to find another way out. We've got Esri behind us."

Tarrys nodded, her eyes worried. "The paths have been feeling familiar to me. I think there's another exit beyond here. But it's just a feeling."

"It's better than nothing." Going forward was a risk. But so was going back. Just because they hadn't seen the Esris' light in a couple of hours didn't mean they weren't still being followed. The Esri could be using the same lighting technique as Tarrys, and probably were. If he had to face them, he'd face them, but strictly as a last resort. They knew he was human and would be going for the jugular. If he killed either of them, which could only be accomplished with fire and the death curse, he'd bring the whole damned Esri race down on his head.

Chapter 12

They hadn't gone far when Charlie found himself reaching for one of the canteens he kept in the vest beneath his tunic. He took a small swig, letting the cool water slide down his parched throat. Thirst was beginning to hound him.

He was tempted to ask her to try to make a spring appear, but he remembered how she'd called for the tree to provide the fruit—with her full palms pressed against the bark. Hitting the crystals in that manner would light them up like the sun, giving away their position. He still had one full canteen and a little water left in a second. At the rate he was going, he'd have both drained in an hour, but by then they might be well clear of the mountain.

Tarrys stopped abruptly and Charlie had to grab her to steady himself, to keep from tipping them both over.

"What's wrong?" He could feel the tension in her slender shoulders. Then, as he looked ahead, he knew. In the dim fingertip of light cast by the crystal he could see two black maws instead of one. This was the first time in a long time they'd come to a choice and the first time at all that she'd hesitated.

"I don't know which one to take."

"You think one of them is the way out?"

"Yes. I'm pretty sure one leaves the mountain and the other goes through. But I don't know which is which."

Charlie reached for her hand, feeling her rising agitation. "Go with your gut."

"My gut?"

"Your instincts. They've led you right this far." But the rueful expression she tossed him made him wonder if she'd been guessing all along. If she truly had no idea where they were, he might be doomed to wander inside these crystal walls until he died of old age. Or black trimor poisoning.

"Let's see if we can make this easy. We'll walk a short way into one of the tunnels and maybe catch a whiff of fresh air or a sound from the outside."

She cocked a skeptical brow. "We're miles inside the mountain."

"Are you one hundred percent sure of that?"

A grimace twisted her lips. "No."

"Then let's give it a try. He tugged her about ten feet into the left tunnel, then wrapped his arm around her waist. But no scent of water tickled his nose. No chirping of birds met his ears. The tunnel felt the same as the original.

"Anything?" he asked, praying something sparked a memory in her.

"No."

He sighed, but refused to be disappointed. Not yet.

"Me either." He led her into the other tunnel and once more stood with her, in silence, hand in hand. "Anything?"

"They're the same," Tarrys said.

But that was just it. They weren't. One meant life. The other almost certain death.

"Decide, Tarrys."

She looked up, meeting his gaze. "My instinct tells me to go right. But I can't tell if that's because that's the way out, or because that's the way I would have gone before, back into the mountain. I honestly don't know and I don't want to choose."

What did his own instincts tell him? He thought about it for a moment and came up with nothing. "Let's go right. Let's follow your first instinct."

Tarrys looked decidedly uneasy. "Okay."

Charlie tugged on her hand and they retraced their steps and continued walking. If he didn't get out of this place soon his back was going to be permanently bowed.

The air between them held a coarse tension, anticipation riddled with anxiety, as they headed into the dark. Though Charlie strained to hear the scream of a flying snake or the scent of trees, mile after mile passed without change. Hope proved harder and harder to hang on to.

They'd walked for hours to get this far, he reminded himself. They might well have to walk for hours to get back out, so there was no sense in getting discouraged.

Easier said than done.

The silence between them began to weigh on him and he decided it was foolish. If they reached the outside, they'd know it when they got there. There was nothing to be gained by listening for the sounds.

"How did you happen to be born in here?" he asked Tarrys.

"My mother was a miner."

His brows lifted. "She mined the crystals?"

"Yes. Before the sealing of the gates, Esria was lit and warmed by the power of the seven stones. When the stones were lost, light crystals became the source of light and warmth in the royal court and most of the wealthy halls. The Marceils were enslaved to serve the Esri and to work the mines. My mother was one of them."

"So there was a whole community of Marceils living in here. Men, women, children?"

"Not children. Only me. The peoples of Esria rarely conceive, especially since the loss of the seven stones. I'd never seen a child until I followed Baleris into your world."

"Never?" He looked at her incredulously.

"No. There were only fifteen miners in this end of the mine. Until I was nine years old, I'd never seen anyone else."

He tried to imagine that, tried to imagine growing up in this darkness, and couldn't manage either one.

"So your father was one of the other miners?"

"I suppose, though *father* isn't a word that has any meaning in this world."

He looked at her askance. "Are you trying

to tell me you don't need two people to reproduce?"

Her mouth quirked up. "Yes, we need two. One of the other miners sired me. But neither Marceils nor Esri mate for life as humans do."

Charlie scoffed. "Believe me, humans don't mate for life."

A frown crossed her pretty face. "Jack and Larsen promised to forsake all others when they married. Do you think they lied?"

"No. They meant it. But despite the good intentions, I've never known a marriage to last."

"None? Truly?"

"Well, I've known some, but they're the exceptions, not the rule."

"Your parents'?"

"My parents' lasted long enough to produce two kids. Then dear old Dad rode into the sunset with a younger model and never looked back. But we weren't talking about my messed-up family. We were talking about yours. So, you didn't know who your father was?"

"No. Among races who rarely conceive,

choosing a single mate is neither necessary nor particularly wise. A female increases her chances of finding the most compatible male for conception if she doesn't limit her number of partners. There were only eight men among the fifteen Marceilian miners. Any one of the eight might have sired me. But it didn't matter. All treated me as a daughter. All the Marceils raised me those first nine years."

"What happened when you were nine?" And why did he get the feeling he wasn't going to like the answer?

"The Esri found out about me."

"They didn't know there was a kid in here for *nine years?*"

"The Esri rarely came far into the mines, disliking the low ceilings as much as you must. They don't need to be present to control their slaves. The Marceils dug for crystals and turned them over to the Esri because they had no choice. If the Esri had known my mother was pregnant, they would have taken me and sold me the moment I was weaned. As it was, I had a chance to know freedom…and what it was like to have a family to love me." Her words trailed off with an ache of loss that pulled at something deep inside him, something he didn't want anything to do with.

"So the Esri finally caught you?"

"It was my fault. The others had told me stories of the outside, stories of winding streams, colorful birds, and a golden sky. I wanted to see them for myself."

Such a simple thing, curiosity. He found himself tensing, suspecting the tragedy that followed.

"Over and over again, I begged my mother to take me outside, but she always refused. She explained why, that there were bad people out there who would steal me away. But I'd never seen an Esri, of course. Even *they* sounded fascinating, in a way. One night I was feeling particularly willful. My mother had scolded me for something—I don't even remember what, now. But I was angry and wanted to get back at her."

Her words fell silent. If there had been light, he was certain he'd find tears in her eyes as she remembered the small rebellion that had cost her everything.

"You left and they caught you," he said quietly.

"Yes. Just as my mother warned, one of the Esri guards saw me and snatched me. I never saw my family again."

He squeezed her hand. "I'm sorry, Tarrys." And he was. He couldn't imagine… No, maybe that was the problem. He *could* imagine. He'd lost his dad just as completely. And though his mom hadn't physically left, she might as well have for all the mothering she'd done after his dad took off.

"Is this the first time you've been back in the mines?"

"Yes."

"I'm sorry. This has to be hard for you."

She lit a dot of light, then glanced back at him, her eyes sad but not damp, a melancholy smile lifting her lips. "I was never happier than those years. Being back reminds me of that. Of the laughter. Of being loved. But it also brings back the harsh regret I've lived with every day since. I keep thinking I'll hear them, that I'll see my mother's face around the next bend, even though I know this mine has been deserted for years."

"Why? It's still full of crystal."

"Crystal, yes, but not light crystals."

"I thought these were all light crystals."

"No, we have to touch these to draw the light. And they provide no warmth. The crystals the Esri seek provide light and warmth without touch. When I was here before, these caves were never dark. The light glowed in rainbows of color all the time. I never realized how beautiful it was until I'd lost it."

They fell back into silence as they continued through the dark labyrinth. At every bend, Charlie prayed for a glimpse of russet or gold sky, or any sign at all that they'd found the way out. Though he tried to ignore his constant thirst, it was starting to drive him crazy.

As he pulled out his canteen, his hands shook like a drunk who had had too much vodka. Though the gentleman inside him told him to offer Tarrys the first sip, his greedy mouth got there first. Sweet water trickled down his throat. It was all he could do to tear the flask away from his lips moments before he drained it. Damn, but he was out of control.

He offered that last sip to Tarrys, perhaps the hardest thing he'd ever done. To his intense and greedy relief she shook her head.

"You need it more than I. The poison's making you thirsty, isn't it?"

"Yeah." If they didn't get out of this godforsaken mine soon, he was going to turn to dust and blow away.

He had to keep his mind off his thirst. Think of something else.

"Have you ever tried to find your mother?" As soon as the words were out, he realized his mistake. "Dumb question. You were enslaved. Of course you couldn't have gone looking for her."

"I couldn't, no. But she was dying. I would have lost her either way."

Charlie blinked. "Dying? I thought… Aren't you immortal?"

"No, Marceils live three or four times as long as humans and heal quickly enough to be virtually indestructible. But we don't live forever. Unlike humans, we don't age continually. We reach full growth and stay that way until the last four or five years of life. Then we deteriorate quickly and die. My mother had begun to age before I left."

"So you'll look twenty for, what, three hundred years?"

Her soft sound of amusement reached him. "I'm afraid so."

"Do you mind if I ask how old you are?"

"Sixty, give or take."

"Damn."

"I'm twice your age, aren't I?"

Charlie snorted. "Don't go there. Don't even go there." There was only so much a man could handle. The fact that the woman he lusted after was older than his mother was best left in the *I'm not thinking about it* file.

They continued on. Time fell away and still there was no change in the smell of the air, no change in the unrelenting darkness. Charlie's steps grew heavier.

"Tarrys. I've got to get water."

"All right." She looked behind him worriedly. "We need to hide the light."

"We'll use my cloak."

"But we'll have to stay here until it dissipates again."

"You bring me water, eaglet, and you'll have a heck of a time prying me away from it again. Staying here a few minutes won't be a problem." He unfastened the cloak and laid it out on the crystal floor between them.

As Tarrys knelt and slid her hands under the fabric, Charlie arched his back, trying to ease the tension. Faint blue light seeped out beneath the black cloak bathing Tarrys's face, revealing lines of worry he knew mirrored his own.

"Provide, oh Esria. Provide water for these

souls." Tarrys's soft words flowed over him like a caress. *"Please,* provide, my Esria."

Over and over she repeated the chant. When her voice began to take on an anxious edge, he knew something was wrong.

"It's not working, is it?"

Tarrys pulled her hands out from under the cloak and sat back on her heels, her teeth worrying her bottom lip. "When I was a child, small pools of water would appear in the floor every now and then for a few hours, then disappear for several days or more. We had what we needed, but no abundance. The land provided. It always provides for the Marceils and the Esri. But we have to ask."

"Then where's the water?"

"I don't know." She grimaced. "I may not be strong enough. I vaguely remember the others gathered in a circle, chanting. If it took all of them to call the water…"

He finished the thought for her. "We're in trouble."

"Maybe. Maybe not. Perhaps I'll be more

successful in another spot." Her eyes turned hard. "I'm not giving up, Charlie. Neither can you."

Forcing the gnawing frustration aside, he nodded. They were stuck in this spot until the light beneath the cloak dissipated.

He sat and pulled her against him, his arm around her shoulders. "I never give up, no matter how hopeless the situation looks. I always make it through somehow. I wouldn't be here if I didn't."

She leaned her head against his shoulder. "I'll be curious to see how we get out of this."

Charlie chuckled and squeezed her shoulder. "That's my girl." From out of nowhere, a sense of rightness enveloped him. As if holding her like this were the most natural thing in the world. As if she belonged to him, and always had.

Tarrys looked up at him in the low light, her eyes wide in her lovely face, and he found himself tumbling into their violet depths.

He hadn't meant to kiss her again, but her chin lifted, her lips parted, and he was helpless to deny himself another taste of her. She met him halfway, pressing her mouth against his, opening her lips, inviting him in, sending hot need flooding his tired body.

As he thrust his tongue into her mouth, she shuddered, moaning with pleasure, and he deepened the kiss as her tongue slid over his in a sinuous dance of welcome. His senses exploded. Colors swirled behind his eyelids. She tasted like heaven.

The rush of blood to his groin hardened him, whipping him loose of his moorings. With frantic need, he pulled her onto his lap and dug his fingers into her hair, slanting his head to deepen the kiss.

She wrenched away and was off his lap so quickly, he barely had time to grab the end of the rope.

"He's calling me!"

The pull of the rope stung his palms as he

gripped it hard and hauled her back onto his lap, struggling to contain her flailing limbs before he took a fist to the jaw. The ceiling was too low to fling her over his shoulder and carry her, so he stayed where he was, determined to hold her tight until the compulsion waned.

The blue glow disappeared, plunging them into darkness, but Tarrys's struggles and groans continued. She wasn't big, but she was strong and it took more effort than he would have thought to contain her constant struggles. He watched that black chasm for sign of their pursuers, but saw no flicker of light.

Tarrys's thrashing didn't abate. He could hear her breaths coming in labored gasps. She was wearing herself out, but it didn't matter. While her Esri master called, she was compelled to answer.

When exhaustion began to stalk him, Charlie knew he was in trouble. He'd never felt anything like it in his life. One moment he was fine, the next moment his limbs felt like they each weighed an extra fifty pounds.

"Tarrys…" Exhaustion sucker punched him, making his head reel. "The poison. Can't fight it."

"I can't go back to him! You need me. Lie on me."

He didn't think twice, just rolled her under him as he collapsed, unable to fight the over-powering weakness.

"Too heavy." He'd crush her.

"No, this is good. You can't hurt me. And I can't get away."

But as the exhaustion pulled him low, he felt her reaching under his tunic.

"Charlie." His name rose an octave from beginning to end. "Charlie, I have your knife. I think he wants me to stab you. Charlie, I'm going to kill you if you don't stop me!"

Her words came to him as if from a distance. *Knife.* She would kill him. Must. Stop. Her. His brain knew the urgency, but his body wouldn't react. *Couldn't* react. Drowning in the poison's sludge, he felt her arm slide out from under him, felt the sting of a knife cut on his hand, and knew she'd pulled the knife free.

No. The cry wrenched from his mind, resonating in his deepest heart. *I refuse to die.*

But he no longer had any more control over his body than Tarrys did hers. As the sludge closed over his head, dragging him into oblivion, he felt the sting of the knifepoint at his throat.

And knew he would never wake up again.

Chapter 13

"Charlie, *stop me!*" Tears ran into Tarrys's hair and sweat soaked her gown as she fought against the Esri's control. As she fought not to kill the man she loved.

But Charlie had collapsed on top of her and his weight now crushed her, the hard crystal floor digging into her back. Her new master must wish her to take Charlie's own weapon and kill him with it because, despite the dead-weight pinning her, she'd managed to steal Charlie's knife from beneath his tunic and now held it, the tip of the blade nicking his throat.

Her muscles strained, bunching, as her mind

desperately fought against the Esri's control of her body. "No," she cried into the empty mine tunnel, her voice echoing off the crystal, ringing back at her with terror. *"I won't. Kill. Him."* The horror of the thought, of ending the life of this beautiful man, thudded in her ears.

Make me do anything but this. Not this.

Her tears ran faster, her teeth grinding to chalk in her mouth as she struggled not to press the blade through his throat. Pain lanced her skull, tracing across the surface like fire. Tremors racked her body.

I won't kill him. I won't kill him. I won't! The fire along her scalp burst, arcing through her in a torrent of heat, a pain that suddenly and profoundly changed to strength and power, rushing through her body, flowing down her arms.

Gritting her teeth in a savage grin, she fought the compulsion to press the knife into his tender, mortal flesh.

I will not kill him!

As the thought roared through her head, something shattered, tearing through her mind.

Her hand flung backward, over her head, the knife clattering on the crystal far behind her head.

I did it.

Tarrys lay beneath Charlie's crushing weight, her heart pounding, her mind in shock.

Sweet Esria, I broke the Esri's control.

That strange heat continued to pound inside her body, beating back the Esri's power, filling her with a startling sense of energy and well-being.

A faint blue glow erupted, shining softly, and she turned her head to look for the crystal she must have accidentally touched. She glanced about in confusion, when she caught sight of her hand.

Thunder pounded in her head as she stared at the glowing blue of her own flesh.

Her jaw dropped, her eyes darting in disbelief. She was the one glowing, not the crystal.

What kind of magic had she tapped?

The moisture in her eyes turned to tears of relief as a soft watery laugh escaped her throat.

For the first time in her life, she'd freed herself from another's control. But had she succeeded in time?

Frantic, she reached for Charlie's neck, suddenly fearful that she'd cut him without realizing, terrified that even as she'd struggled for freedom, she'd sent Charlie into the waiting arms of death.

Charlie woke with a start, his senses roaring to life at the feel of a soft body beneath his, a softer hand sliding down his throat. Tarrys's sweet scent filled his senses.

Jesus, he must be crushing her. He levered himself up and onto his elbows, lifting his head to peer down into her face.

Her *glowing* face.

His eyes went wide. *Holy crap.* Chills snaking up his back, he levered himself off her in a single lunge to crouch warily at her side. He knew she wasn't human, but *Jesus.*

From that glowing blue face she grinned at him, her eyes soft with relief. "You're okay."

"You're glowing." Her face, her neck, her hands.

Her smile dimmed as she sat up, her dark hair swinging around her shoulders and into her face.

Her hair.

Chills raced over his skin. "How many days have I been out?"

Tarrys's eyes must have grown as wide as his own as she reached up and touched the thick, wavy locks that fell nearly to her shoulders. "Minutes. You were only out minutes."

"No way." His mind scrabbled for purchase, struggling to stop this free fall into the twilight zone. "What happened? The last thing I remember, I was falling on top of you. I felt a knife at my throat."

"I tried to kill you." She flinched. "Not willingly." Both of her hands went to her head, her fingers touching her hair, sliding down the silken locks as if feeling them for the very first time.

And she was.

Her gaze swung to his, wonder and triumph in her violet eyes. "I fought him, Charlie. I won."

He stared at her as understanding ripped through the shock that clouded his brain. "You broke his control?"

The grin on her face returned, wider than before. "I can still feel him commanding me to kill you." She dropped her hands, her head shaking slowly back and forth. "But I feel no need to respond."

"That's great," he murmured, sitting back hard, struggling to take it all in.

Tarrys was a…revelation. The hair swinging around her pretty face was lovely, but it was the joy lighting her eyes, the power radiating through the confident smile lifting her lips that made her extraordinary, beautiful in a way he'd never seen her before.

But even as he stared at her, her smile died, her brows drawing together.

"What's the matter?" His gaze followed hers to a small, smooth crevice in the crystal wall.

"I know this place." Dismay colored her voice.

And he was all too afraid he understood. "We went the wrong way, didn't we?"

The blue glow of her skin faded to nothing, casting them into the dark. A fingertip of green light lit the wall behind her.

"Yes." The word was little more than a hard exhalation.

The full extent of the error slowly crashed over him. They weren't nearing an exit, but heading deeper into the mountain. With no water. No antidote to the poison.

"Let me try to call the water again," she said softly.

"We haven't gone far from where you tried it the last time."

"No. But I feel stronger." But as she reached for his cloak, she stilled suddenly, her eyes widening.

"What is it, Tarrys?" Charlie asked softly.

Her gaze darted left and right. "My master."

"Do you hear him?"

"No." The gaze she snapped to his was filled with wonder. "I know where he is. Where they both are."

"How?"

"I don't know. I've never been able to sense my masters like this before. But I sense him clearly, and he's not alone."

"Where are they, then?"

"More than a mile behind us. And not moving."

"They're probably resting." He lifted an eyebrow. "You're sure about this?" His brain wanted to scoff, but he'd seen too much magic to truly doubt anything at this point.

"Positive." The gaze that met his flashed with certainty, mirroring the tone of her voice. "I know precisely where he is."

"That's good. They may be able to track us, but now we can track them, too." Still, as he considered their situation, he frowned. "That fork in the road was well over a mile back."

"I know. We can't go that way. We're going to have to go through the mountain, now."

They looked at each other, silence stretching between them on a thin wire of tension. "I'll get you water, Charlie. I promise."

The earnest sincerity that flared in her eyes moved him. He'd promised her he'd get her to safety. Now she was doing the same.

The question was—could either of them succeed?

She turned toward the wall, her thick hair sweeping over her shoulders. "Ready? It's going to be bright."

With their pursuers more than a mile back, and trackable, there was no longer any need to hide the light. Charlie braced himself for the blinding glow as Tarrys pressed her palms flat against the crystal wall. Green light burst through the tunnel, releasing the scent of mushrooms.

"Provide, my Esria," she murmured, her voice trembling with emotion. "I beg you, provide for these souls."

Almost at once, Charlie felt something

change in the air and heard a hum, like that of electricity. And the sound of...*water.*

Tarrys whirled toward him, her wide-eyed gaze plowing into him. "Do you hear that?" Excitement flushed her face, filling him with raw hope and a nearly unbearable need to touch her.

"You did it." He grabbed her face between his hands and kissed her hard.

Tarrys pulled back, her expression at once triumphant and uncertain. "Let's see if I really produced anything useful before we celebrate." She turned and he followed her toward the darkness beyond and the sound of trilling birds.

The unmistakable scent of water reached his nose, twisting his thirst into painful knots. As they rounded the corner, Tarrys hit the wall with her palm and light erupted on a sight that brought her up short and nearly knocked him back on his heels.

Before them lay an oasis—a crystal rainbow of a room with a soaring ceiling, a tree that stood more than twenty feet tall and hung heavy with fruit, and a wide pool of clear water surrounded by thick gold-and-orange grass dotted with tiny pink flowers.

A miracle.

Charlie stepped forward, straightening with a sigh, able to stand upright for the first time since entering the mine. He turned and grabbed Tarrys, lifting her and swinging her high as relief and gratitude burst from his pores like bubbles of champagne.

Tarrys's eyes glittered with moisture, her laughter ringing as sweetly as bells, echoing off the high crystal like chimes on Easter morning. Charlie caught her against him and kissed her, claiming her smile, pressing his mouth to hers for one precious moment before releasing her.

As much as he needed her, he needed the water more. The last thing he wanted was for this oasis to turn into a mirage before he ever got a sip.

"Drink," she urged, as if sharing his thought.

He lunged for the pool and sank to his knees beside its banks, scooping handful after handful of the cool water into his mouth. His eyes glazed over as the precious wetness coated his tongue then slid coolly down his throat. Never had anything tasted so good.

When he didn't think his stomach could hold another drop, he dunked his face, scrubbing the sweat and travel grit off his skin. But when he looked up again, the sight that met his eyes had the breath catching in his throat.

Tarrys had stripped off her slave's gown and was wading into the water, perfectly, gloriously nude. The blue-green light from the crystal below her feet illuminated that perfect body for him all over again.

His pulse skipped and began to race. His blood heated and pooled between his legs. "Where are the Esri? Are they moving yet?"

Her gaze lifted and met his, something hot leaping between them. "No. We're alone."

His heart thudded as he reached for the clasp of his cloak.

Chapter 14

As Tarrys met Charlie's heated gaze, she felt the desire arc between them, felt it in the tightening of her breasts and the flushing of her skin. She watched as Charlie removed his cloak, pounding excitement warring with fluttering uncertainty inside her. She hadn't meant to offer herself to him, had really only meant to take a much-needed bath until their gazes met, igniting a need that would not be ignored.

She wanted this, longing to share everything she was, everything she had, with this man— her newfound power, her joy, her love.

Charlie stripped off the silver tunic and unfastened the laden gear vest he wore beneath.

The thought of mating with him made her pulse leap until it was pounding in her throat. Why? Mating had never been anything but the relief of a violent need, a need forced on her by another. Yet this felt different, a wanting as much of the heart as of the body. Strong and seductive, this longing called to her, cajoling instead of demanding. And her body answered, craving his touch, his kiss, and anything else he wanted to give her.

The thought of just exactly what he wanted to give her made her body weep in dark, secret places. As Charlie removed his military vest and laid it on the grass, she sank down until the water caressed her shoulders, cooling her heated skin. She watched him, unable to tear her gaze away, as he stripped off his T-shirt. Her breath caught at the sheer beauty of his masculine body. Esri were slender with little musculature. And the few humans she'd seen without shirts last summer in D.C. had been soft with fat or skinny as Esri.

Charlie Rand was neither. His shoulders were

broad, his arms and chest thickly muscled, his waist trim and hard. Wearing only his borrowed silken Esri pants and boots, he pulled his water flasks out of his vest, filled them, then drank them down one after the other.

As he filled them again, he glanced at her with a grin and a shrug. "In case this miracle doesn't last."

Tarrys smiled, his grin loosening the last of her reserve. Love welled up inside her, thick and strong, misting her eyes.

He returned the full water flasks to his vest, then met her gaze and held it as he pulled off his boots, then slowly removed his pants. The evidence of his arousal sent a shudder of pleasure arcing through her at the heady realization that although she might be a slave to her desire for him, he was equally a slave to his desire for her. The thought made her smile with a feeling of rightness and strength, with a power that had nothing to do with the energy that allowed her to free herself from the Esri's control. And everything to do with love.

Charlie entered the pond, walking slowly toward her, making her pulse accelerate at an alarming rate. Her breathing turned labored, her throat constricted by aching anticipation as she waited for him to reach her and take her into his arms.

But instead of swooping in to claim her as she expected him to, he stopped a few feet in front of her, his gaze questioning. Searching.

He was asking for permission to touch her, she realized. *Asking.*

Love for him overwhelmed her. Tears sprang up in her eyes and she closed the distance between them, the cool water sloshing against her heated thighs as she moved. Charlie watched her, his eyes hot as fire and soft with tenderness as she laid her palm on his chest. Excitement ripped through her, but still he didn't take what she offered.

Instead, he cupped her face in his broad hands. "Are you sure?"

"Yes. I've never been more sure of anything."

"Good." He grinned, making her laugh, then

cut off her laughter as he pulled her into his arms and covered her mouth in a kiss as hard as it was tender, as fierce as it was gentle.

The feel of his tongue sliding into her mouth, his muscled chest against the tips of her breasts, his hard erection high on her abdomen, sent her senses spinning. This passion was like nothing in her experience. Exquisitely pleasurable. Gloriously perfect.

Charlie gripped her waist and lifted her until they were eye to eye. Without hesitation, she spread her thighs, hooking her legs around his waist until his erection pressed against her sensitive flesh.

Excitement arced, and a need so fierce she could hardly stand it. Her hands dug into his hair as his mouth slanted over hers, inhaling her as she inhaled him. Closer. She needed him closer.

Holding her in his arms, Charlie walked to the center of the pond until the water lapped at their waists. Then he sank until the water reached her shoulders and she was straddling his lap.

Pulling away, he looked at her, really looked at her. His gaze delved into her with an intensity that made her heart pound.

"You are so beautiful," he murmured, his eyes gleaming.

Sweet Esria, but she loved him.

He leaned toward her and kissed her again, as if he couldn't get enough of her, his tongue diving in to meld with her own. As he kissed her, his hands gripped her waist and he lifted her and lowered her in the water, rubbing her against the length of his arousal, driving her to a frenzy of wanting. She circled his neck, pressing her breasts against his chest, rocking her hips. The water splashed between them.

"Do you want me?" Charlie said against her mouth.

"Yes."

"Hold your breath." He fell back, pulling her with him underwater. As his tongue dove into her mouth, he lifted her hips and pushed himself deep inside her, filling her in ways no man ever had. Filling her body, her heart, her soul.

She knew nothing in her life had ever been so right. And feared it would never be again.

Chapter 15

Charlie reared up out of the water, pulling Tarrys with him, lifting her hips, then pulling them down again, driving himself deeper inside her with every plunge. Her head was thrown back, her face a mask of intense pleasure, mirroring the incredible sensations spearing him. The feel of her was like nothing he'd ever known. Every stroke, every thrust rushed through him on a wave of pleasure almost as intense as a full-blown orgasm.

Tenderness built like a pressure in his chest. The sweet grip of her hands at the back of his neck, the brush of her soft breasts against his chest. He wanted to come inside her over and over again and never let her go. The slender expanse of her neck beckoned and he had to taste it. With a sudden certainty, he knew he'd die if he didn't have his mouth on her somewhere.

He kissed her throat, then the underside of her chin, then her cheek, drawing her heavy-lidded gaze to his. Sweet heaven, she was an angel. His mouth captured hers as he continued to drive into her, swallowing the small moans and gasps that rose on soft bursts from her throat. Colors exploded behind his eyelids, brighter and brighter with every thrust until they were more brilliant than a rainbow, more beautiful than a thousand crystal mines in full glow.

And still he drove into her.

Her moans rose to shouts of desperate need as she clung to him, her fingers digging into his hair. Each plunge into her depths thrust him higher and higher until he wondered if the building explosion would be enough to send the mines crumbling around them. He didn't care. Need raged until he was so far past anything in his experience he no longer knew what to expect.

Tarrys's cries buffeted him like driving winds, tearing him loose from his moorings. Her heart pounded in sync with his as if they'd merged into one tempest. One being. It was a good thing their pursuers were more than a mile back.

Her cries rose, quicker, faster, and he knew she was near the peak. As the triumphant cry of her release echoed off the crystal, her deep inner contractions pulled him toward his own, urging him to set himself free, to give himself up to the chaos of the storm.

No.

Deep inside, something rebelled, fighting for control. Fighting off the chaos.

As his own climax crashed upon him, Charlie opened his eyes, jerking back to himself as he fixed on the pleasure of the release pounding through his body, rejecting the pull of the tempest. When his passion was spent, he held

Tarrys against him, their hearts thundering out of sync.

Holding her, he felt oddly alone. As if she'd ridden the storm and left him behind. As if, at that critical moment, they'd become two instead of one.

Two was good. Jesus, he didn't want to be one. Not with anyone.

But he didn't let her go. Instead, he stroked her wet back, the water lapping gently around them, as the aftershocks of the most cataclysmic sexual encounter of his life rolled through his body.

It was just sex, he tried to tell himself. But he knew better. He'd had more partners than he cared to remember, yet never had he experienced anything even remotely like this. The other encounters might as well have never happened.

Tarrys's hands slid into his hair. She lifted her head and met his gaze, those eyes pulling him down into their warm violet depths.

Slowly, she leaned forward and kissed him tenderly on the cheek.

"I love you, Charlie Rand."

Her words went through him like a shot, ripping away the last of the lingering pleasure riding his body. *Love.* If there was one thing that could ruin a private moment for him, it was talk of love—the nail in the coffin of any relationship. The moment his partner-of-the-moment started making noises about feelings or futures, he was gone. Except, dammit, where in the hell was he going to go?

He released her, pulling out of her slowly, his body resisting the separation even as his mind rejected the fierce need to hold her. Setting Tarrys on her feet in the water beside him, he stood.

"We need to get going." His tone was sharp, his words gruff, but he didn't care. Her words had thrown him off balance.

As he strode across the crystal to retrieve his clothes, the lights gleamed beneath his feet. With swift, frustrated movements, he jerked his pants up his wet legs then returned to the pool to rinse out his sweaty T-shirt.

Tarrys was kneeling before the far wall, her palms pressed against twin circles of glowing yellow.

"Oh Esria, please provide the carnasserie bush we need to cure Charlie's poison. I beg you, *provide.*" Water droplets ran from her wet hair down her straight, slender back, glistening in the crystal's glow.

Something warm and painful stabbed him in the chest as he watched her kneeling in supplication, praying to this world he didn't understand, *for him.*

She glanced over her shoulder, looking around, then stood on a sigh. "I didn't really think it would work." Picking up her gown, she walked to the pool. "The land provides sustenance. Food, water. Nothing so specific as a carnasserie bush, but it was worth a try."

Tarrys dunked her gown in the water, rinsing it out on the far side of the pool from where he did the same with his shirt. He struggled to keep his gaze on his task and off her seductively bare curves even as he tried to forget the L-word she'd uttered.

"How are you feeling?" Her eyes, when she glanced at him were warm with concern, but revealed nothing of the emotion she claimed to feel. Maybe she thought *I love you* was the proper way to end lovemaking for a human. The thought almost eased his mind.

"I'm fine." He frowned, thinking about it. "I actually feel better than I have for days."

She smiled gently. "I'm glad. I wonder if my newfound power is helping you, too."

He followed her train of thought. "You think you might have healed me?" With the sex? Marvin Gaye's voice floated through his mind. *Sexual healing.*

Tarrys shrugged. "I don't know. It might not last." She pulled her gown from the water and wrung it out, twisting the fabric into a pretzel.

Her gaze snapped to his, suddenly, and she leaped to her feet in a single graceful move. "The Esri are moving again. I can feel them."

"We'd better get going, then."

They dressed quickly, Charlie donning his gear, Esri tunic and cloak, as before.

"Are we going through the mountain?" Tarrys asked as her wet gown settled around her ankles.

He pulled on his tunic. "The only alternative is to go back the way we came. To fight the Esri."

"Yes."

He sighed, itching for that fight and knowing it could only end badly. Now that Tarrys was able to call food and water, and couldn't be controlled, there was no choice. Even if the poison eventually got him, she'd be able to get away.

"We'll go through the mountain."

Tarrys nodded. "I agree."

As they ducked back into the dark tunnel, Charlie hoped they weren't making a grave mistake.

Tarrys glanced back to where Charlie followed in the narrowing tunnel. The low ceiling forced him to bend even lower than before, but he saw her turn and looked up, meeting her gaze with warm, if somewhat guarded, eyes. Love for him welled up inside her, overwhelming and confusing.

So much had happened in the last hours. Too much to wrap her mind around. Not only had she managed to break free of an Esri's control for the first time in her life, but she'd also inexplicably acquired power she'd never had.

Yet the thing that sang clearest in her heart was that Charlie had made love to her and that mating had been like nothing she'd ever experienced. With him, she'd found a closeness she'd never imagined possible. A beautiful sharing of passion and pleasure, of bodies and emotions.

She felt as if she'd seen into his heart. His soul.

But he didn't seem to feel the same.

As the climax had come over her, she'd felt him pulling back. Not physically, but emotionally. As if he hadn't meant to get that close. Hadn't wanted to.

Perhaps this was typical with humans. Sharing their bodies with another was not something they did easily or simply. She knew that. Perhaps this awkwardness after was usual. Or perhaps she'd somehow displeased him, though she couldn't imagine how that could be. He'd reached his pleasure, she was certain of that. And he was feeling better. They'd been traveling for hours since they made love and he had yet to show any sign of weakening. He didn't even seem to be overly thirsty.

A bright and newfound optimism lived inside her, now. A hope that with her sudden power she might actually be able to get Charlie through Esria safely.

That's all she wanted, all she'd ever wanted. Marceils knew better than to dream.

"Where are the Esri?" Charlie asked, not bothering to crane his neck to try to meet her gaze. She couldn't imagine how uncomfortable he must be, forced to travel so many miles in such a position.

"A little more than half a mile back," Tarrys told him. "They're moving faster than we are, now."

"Crap. Then I'd better step it up. Let me lead for a while since I'm the one slowing us down."

Charlie gripped her shoulders and edged past her, careful not to touch her any more than he had to. As if touching her was no longer pleasant. Tarrys tried not to care.

Moments later, as they came around the next curve, Charlie stopped so suddenly she ran into him.

"Dammit to hell," he muttered.

"What's the matter?" Tarrys held on to his hips and peered around him.

The sight that met her gaze sent her heart plummeting. A dead end. And they hadn't passed another fork in the road for miles.

The Esri were behind them. There was no escape.

Charlie turned to face her, then sank to his

knees and arched his back, his expression grim as he met her gaze.

Tarrys raked her hair back from her face. "What are we going to do?"

His mouth compressed. "There's only one thing we can do, now. Prepare to fight."

Chapter 16

Charlie knelt on the crystal floor as he faced the dark tunnel from which they'd just come. There was no sign of light—no sign of the Esri. Yet. But they were coming. And there was no escape.

He'd been itching for this battle for the past couple of days, from the moment one of the bastards had tried to rape Tarrys. But now that it was upon him, his battle lust had turned to dread. Dread that he wouldn't be able to keep Tarrys safe.

She might not be controlled at the moment, but he had no confidence she'd remain free if they caught her again. She'd told him that the first thing the Esri did to a newly captured slave was cut off her hair.

He was beginning to suspect the Marceils were like Samson, their power in their locks. And if so, would she lose that power, and her freedom, if her hair was stolen again?

He refused to let that happen.

Yet how was he supposed to keep her safe and at the same time fight two armed, indestructible immortals while hunched over like a hundred-year-old man?

If only he dared kill the bastards. *That* he could accomplish with fire and the death chant. He'd packed two small flamethrowers and half a dozen lighters for just such a situation.

The problem was, the moment he killed even one, he'd be marked for death with a magical X flashing his whereabouts on every map in Esria. As tempting as it might be to eliminate this pair for eternity, doing so would seal his and Tarrys's fate. Not his best option.

"He's calling me," Tarrys said softly.

Charlie looked at her. "Do I need to tie you?"

"No, but I think I should go to him anyway."

"Negative." His hand hooked around her upper arm. "You're not going anywhere near that bastard."

She met his gaze, hard determination in her eyes. "It's a good plan, Charlie. They'll think I'm controlled, so they won't be watching for my attack. I might be able to help you."

"No."

"Charlie…"

"Have you forgotten you have hair? The first thing they'll do is chop it off, then you *will* be controlled. I'm right, aren't I?"

"I don't know." But the truth was in her eyes.

"I think you do. They're not touching you, Tarrys." The thought of what they'd nearly done to her made him insane. "You're staying behind me."

She crossed her arms, temper glittering in her eyes. "I thought I was your partner."

"You are."

Leaning forward until they were eye to eye,

her stance was aggressive enough to heat his blood, and not with temper. Until she clapped her hands together an inch from his nose, making him jerk back and bump his head on the ceiling, dammit.

"Get your priorities straight, Charlie. You *must* get by those two Esri without killing them if you want to save your world. I'm not asking you to leave me behind. I'm demanding you use what may be your only advantage in this fight—the fact that they think they control me...and don't."

"They may know you're not controlled the moment they see that hair."

"That's a chance we have to take."

Clearly she didn't get it. He gripped her head between his hands and leaned in until they were nearly nose to nose.

"They'll try to rape you."

"So? It's not like human rape. They won't hurt me."

"How do you know that? They're more than capable of hurting you."

"It doesn't matter. I'll heal." Her hands slid to his unshaven face, her expression softening. "You're a fine man, Charlie. It's in your nature to protect the weak. But I'm not weak. I'm a weapon that might give you the advantage you need to win this battle."

He stared into her eyes, *drowned* in the depths of them, and knew from the strength he saw in them that she spoke the truth.

"Charlie, if you lose, if they kill you, what do you think I'll be facing then?"

She was right. Everything she said was right. Yet putting her in danger went against every instinct he possessed. Then again, he'd be right behind her. They wouldn't get their pants untied before he beat the crap out of them.

"All right."

Satisfaction lit Tarrys's eyes and she nodded, sure and fearless as she released him and stepped back. "Break their bones. Their necks sometimes take the longest to heal. The more bones you break, the longer they'll be down. If you can, tie them with your rope. That might slow them more."

He saluted her. "Yes, ma'am." And he wasn't kidding. The woman knew what she was doing. But letting her go to those monsters, letting her walk right into their hands, was going to kill him. Reaching for her, he pulled her to him and pressed his mouth to hers, needing to feel her against him one more time. *Mine.* The word rolled through him, filling him with the fierce need to claim her…to brand her as his.

He finally drew back and slipped a thick lock of hair behind her ear. "Be careful."

Her eyes searched his, worry swirling in their depths. "You, too. Charlie…" Again, she pressed her palms to his cheek. "They can't hurt me, no matter what it looks like. Remember that."

"I'll try."

A smile flickered over her features. With a quick roll of her eyes, she turned and ran lightly down the tunnel, away from him.

Slowly, he rose to his feet, giving her a head

start. Then, pulse leaping into a hard battle pound, he took off after her. He'd run only a couple of minutes when he heard them.

"Watch your back for the Sitheen," one of the Esri shouted. "It's a setup. She's not controlled."

Charlie's blood went cold. They knew.

"What do you mean?" asked a second voice. "What are you doing?"

"Cutting off her hair."

Jesus.

Charlie's muscles bunched as he ran full bore down the winding tunnel until finally the passage curved and he could see them. Tarrys struggled to elude capture as one Esri, the one who'd nearly raped her, lunged for her with a knife.

The second Esri faced Charlie, his face long, his gold eyes gleaming with malice. From one long-fingered hand hung a wicked-looking short sword glistening in the crystal's light. His gaze shifted to Charlie, no surprise evidence in his expression as he pushed past his compatriot to meet Charlie's headlong attack.

In a single move, Charlie pulled his own knife, steel ringing against steel as he parried blow for blow. Perspiration dampened his brow as he fought the skilled swordsman. Charlie's only chance of reaching Tarrys lay in disarming the Esri so that he could break his bones.

"You were a fool to enter this world, human. *Sitheen,*" the Esri sneered, lunging. "I'll end your life quickly."

Charlie fought with everything he had, slashing through the Esri's wrist. The man should have dropped the sword, but the thin line of blood disappeared almost as quickly as it appeared and the Esri only laughed.

Beyond, Tarrys fought her own battle, dodging the knife that would steal that glorious hair of hers and along with it, her freedom.

Dammit. He had to reach her.

The Esri in front of him lunged. Seeing his chance, Charlie used the man's momentum against him, grabbing his wrist and pulling him off balance. In a quick, vicious move, he broke that pale wrist. The Esri's blade clattered to the floor.

But as Charlie reached out to break the Esri's neck, he felt the slap of a hand to the back of his head. Pain detonated like a grenade, blasting away his mind, all sound, thought and feeling.

God help him.

He could feel his energy draining, as if the pain were sucking the very life out of him. Real fear swirled, bloodred, through the agony. If he collapsed now, it was over.

Fighting with every last scrap of strength he possessed, Charlie wrenched himself free of the Esri's hold, hurling himself out of the grip of that agony only to bang his head on the roof of the tunnel as he stumbled backward.

As his spiraling vision cleared, he saw Tarrys and watched with horror as the Esri's knife swung down, taking a chunk of her scalp. Her scream broke through the roar in his head as blood began to stream down her face.

Fury became a fire in his veins.

His own Esri attacker had retrieved his short sword and was lunging for him again. With focused savagery, Charlie met him halfway, slashing the sword and several fingers from the immortal's hand. The Esri yelled, clamping what was left of his bloody appendage around Charlie's wrist, sending that fiery pain shooting up his arm and into his body to spread through his chest. He could barely breathe, and didn't care. Only one thing mattered.

Tarrys.

Digging for every ounce of strength he still possessed, he lowered his shoulder to the center of the Esri's chest and shoved hard, knocking the man back, ramming him into his companion. As he tackled both of the slighter men to the floor, he reached under his tunic and pulled out his small flamethrower.

His brain swam with agony. But as the fire licked out from the flamethrower against the bloody remains of a hand that still gripped him, the words to the death chant came to him in a rush, rolling off his tongue.

The Esri screamed and released him, but it was too late. The fire engulfed both immortal males, immobilizing them in a perfect, if unnatural, arc.

Charlie rolled away, lurching to where Tarrys sagged against the wall, drenched in her own blood. Tears streaked her cheeks, her mouth open as if in a silent scream. A scream that tore through his head.

As he sang the words of the death chant, he grabbed her at the waist and hauled her away from the Esri and away from the fire. Sinking to the ground, he held her against his chest, her mutilated head brushing his chin.

Dear God.

But he continued to chant. His vision spun, his words slurring even as the pain slowly receded from his head to settle in the pit of his heart. As he sank to the floor, Tarrys in his arms, his enemies' bodies began to sparkle with a thousand iridescent lights, lights that slowly rose, hovering above them for one breathless instant before exploding in the narrow space. As the lights erupted like fireworks, the Esri's bodies crumbled, their immortal existence ending in a single pile of ash.

"Oh, Charlie," Tarrys breathed, her voice soft, but strong. "That wasn't good."

She turned on his lap to face him, her face bloody, her scalp already almost fully healed. Her hair remained long and untouched except for the single chunk of bald spot halfway between her temple and her crown, a spot the size of an egg.

He gripped her shoulders and stared into her face, disbelieving. "You're all right?"

"Yes, of course. Are you?"

"You scared the crap out of me."

She glanced back at the pile of ash. "You killed them."

"It was them or us."

She nodded, tears springing to her eyes. With a shudder, she wrapped her arms around his neck and tucked her face against him. Charlie pulled her tight, his hand burrowing into her hair as relief tore through him. He closed his eyes and drank in the feel of her warm weight against his heart. Holding her felt right. Perfect. He was beginning to need her in ways he didn't understand and didn't want to contemplate.

"I was so scared," she murmured against his throat. "I heard you yell. I thought he was going to kill you."

"He packed a wallop with his hand."

"Pain?"

"Yeah." He stroked her head, careful to avoid the wounded patch, though he knew it was fully healed. "Do you still feel your power?"

"I think so. I don't think he took enough of my hair for me to lose it. Do you want me to call for water?"

"Soon." He pulled her back against him, not ready to let her go. "I've got a death mark," he said finally, forcing himself to say the words out loud.

"Yes." Tarrys sighed deeply. "They'll come

for you, of course, but it will take a while. There are no villages in this part of Esria. But they'll follow you now, as easily as my master followed me."

He stroked her hair. "What do you think, should we continue through the mountain or try to backtrack out and go over instead?"

"Through. I know I've made some mistakes, but I believe it'll be quicker and safer to stay in the mountain. The Esri aren't likely to come in after you."

"They'll be waiting for me at the entrance."

"Perhaps, but only if there are travelers nearby, and that isn't likely. I think we can be out of the mountain in under two weeks and there's no village that close. The only problem might be..." She pulled back to look at him.

"What?"

Worry lit her eyes. "The king has horses. The royal court is far, but on horseback, they'll travel much faster. Possibly within that two weeks."

"It's going to be close, then."

"Yes."

"We'd better get moving." He ran his thumb down her bloody cheek. "Do you want a bath before we go?"

A small fire lit deep in her eyes. "I don't think there's time."

Charlie smiled wryly. "There's time if I don't join you." He gave her a quick kiss, then lifted her from his lap.

His body rebelled against letting her go, but now wasn't the time for more intimate pursuits. Besides, he wasn't ready to make love to her again. Sex with Tarrys was too complicated, too…everything.

The woman thought she was in love with him.

And it didn't matter that he was starting to have feelings for her—soft, warm, wildly protective feelings.

Charlie Rand didn't do love.

Chapter 17

Two days later, Tarrys was leading the way through the low, cramped tunnel, lighting the crystals with frequency and impunity. But as she turned yet another corner and slapped her hand against the cool, hard wall, the light flew into darkness.

She stopped abruptly.

"Whoa," Charlie muttered, bumping into her and gripping her shoulder to keep from knocking her down. "What's the matter?"

"Do you smell that?"

Charlie pressed against her back, then pulled

her behind him. "Water. We found the way out."

"No, we couldn't have. We're deep in the heart of the mountain."

"Are you sure?"

"Positive. Light more crystal, Charlie."

Charlie edged forward, slapping his palm against the walls in half a dozen places, but the light couldn't penetrate the darkness ahead.

Tarrys gripped his waist. "Let me go first. I think I might know where we are."

"Tell me." But when she pushed past him, he let her go.

"Better yet, I'll show you." Little by little, she eased her way carefully forward, to the very edge of the darkness, until the wall of the tunnel ended abruptly. Sliding her hand around the curve, she pressed, sending the light outward, beyond the tunnel for the first time. Lighting a wondrous sight.

"Holy cow," Charlie murmured. Joining her, he reached up, lighting the outer wall around the edges of the tunnel in a dozen places, sending light cascading outward in a glorious rainbow to illuminate a huge crystal cavern that, at once, ran far below their cliff-side perch, and soared high above.

A stream ran through the middle, flanked on either side by tall grasses alive with colorful frogs and small birds of pure white.

"Amazing." Charlie took her hand. "Let's hope we can find a path down there from here."

Tarrys edged out to where she could see clearly and quickly spied what appeared to be stairs cut into the crystal. How many Marceils had come through here in the past?

"This way." She started down the stairs, moving as quickly as she dared, her now bare feet lighting each step along the way.

"How long is this cavern, any idea?" Charlie asked behind her. "The light doesn't penetrate that far."

"I don't know. Miles, I think."

"Good. We'll make better time if I can walk upright."

Tarrys glanced at him. "How well do you run?"

He grinned at her. "Damn well."

The faster they made it through the mountain, the better their chance of reaching the Forest of Nightmares before the Esri caught them.

At the base of the stairs, the cavern floor stretched out, smooth and wide, soft ground instead of hard crystal.

"You set the pace," Charlie told her, and she did, her legs having to work harder to keep up with Charlie's longer stride.

For more than an hour, they ran, the cavern showing no sign of ending. Finally, Charlie pulled up.

"I need water."

Tarrys glanced at him, not liking the sudden redness of his face or the perspiration running from his temples. She'd pushed him too hard.

"You should have told me to slow down," she chided.

He said nothing, just collapsed gracelessly

onto his knees beside the stream as if he'd expended his last ounce of energy.

Her heart clenched with the certainty that a healthy Charlie would have been able to keep up that run for hours. Though she'd hoped her newfound power had somehow cured him of the poison, it was clear they hadn't been that lucky. And they were still days, if not weeks, away from reaching the antidote.

Kneeling beside him, she pressed her palms to the floor, begging the land to provide food, then sat back on her heels, waiting…praying… for a response. To her relief, a fruit tree appeared, as before. Charlie was too busy scooping handfuls of water into his mouth to notice.

Tarrys plucked a pair of fruit and joined him, dangling her feet in the water as she took a bite. As he splashed water on his face and scrubbed his skin with his hands, she looked for signs of mottling. And while she saw none, she knew it could appear at any time.

Charlie shook the water from his hair and

glanced at her, eyeing her fruit suspiciously. "It's black."

She swallowed the tangy bite. "It's good," she countered, and tossed him the second one.

Charlie turned the round globe over in his hand. "Looks rotten."

Tarrys rolled her eyes. "In your world black might mean rotten. Here it just means black. Eat it."

With a grimace, he bit into the fruit, made a sound of appreciation and devoured the rest.

Things had changed between them over the past couple of days. The tension and need to drive through the mountain as quickly as possible had obviously worn on Charlie, turning him more moody than she'd seen him. More withdrawn.

She supposed a death mark would do that.

Yet it saddened her, too. The closeness that had been growing between them had fallen away. Charlie rarely looked at her anymore. He hardly even met her gaze, as if even that small connection was more than he wanted with her.

She told herself it was the worry eating at him. That their mating wasn't at the root of his withdrawal. But she wasn't so sure.

Which made what she had to say to him all the more difficult.

Tarrys took a deep breath. "Charlie, I think the poison's back. I think it's time I shared my power with you again."

He glanced at her, wariness in his eyes. "And just how would you do that?"

"You know."

The knowledge flared in his eyes, then disappeared with a scowl. "I'm fine."

But they both knew that was a lie.

The knot of disappointment that had lodged itself beneath her rib cage a couple of days ago grew larger and more painful. If only she knew how she'd displeased him. Because being with him had been the most extraordinary experience, and she desperately wanted to repeat it.

But Charlie had made it clear he didn't feel the same. And that hurt.

She tossed her head, feeling the heavy weight

of hair brush her shoulders. It was funny, really. In the human realm, she'd wished she had long, thick hair, thinking Charlie might be more likely to notice her if she had. But now that she suddenly had thick tresses, he barely looked at her at all.

She stared down into the water, kicking her feet slowly back and forth. "Would you like to try another fruit?"

When he didn't answer, she glanced at him, then watched with alarm as his body began to collapse.

"Charlie!"

Tarrys grabbed for him as he tipped forward and fell into the shallow stream in a boneless heap.

Pulse pounding, she leaped in after him and yanked his head above the water. Humans had to breathe or they drowned. "Charlie, wake up!"

As she stared into his unconscious face, she saw the mottling pattern rising from his neck to his face, darkening by the second.

Fear was a vise, crushing her ribs. Struggling and panting, Tarrys hooked her arms beneath his and backed him out of the water, sliding him up the bank until he lay on the grass. She didn't know if he was breathing, didn't know how to make him start breathing if he'd stopped. She only knew one way to share her power with him and hoped that would be enough.

With shaking hands, she untied his soaked pants and reached inside to free his penis only to find it soft and flaccid. Reaching for it, she began to stroke the damp flesh, eliciting a groan from him that sputtered into a cough.

"Charlie?"

He said nothing, showing no sign of waking, but the worst of her fear slipped away with the proof that he was still alive, still breathing.

Slowly, the flesh beneath her hand began to harden, her soft ministrations awakening her need for him as much as his for her. By the time he was hard enough, she was damp and ready.

Tarrys pulled off her gown, then bent and kissed his unresponsive lips. "I love you, Charlie Rand." She rose and straddled him, guiding him into her damp heat. Pleasure tore through her as she took him deep inside and she gasped and threw her head back, absorbing the rush of passion. His sudden thrust against her startled her. Her head snapped forward until she was staring into heated eyes in a face devoid of the poison's mottling.

Like something out of his fantasies, Charlie woke to find Tarrys straddling him, *riding* him, drawing him deep into her body with velvet strokes of wickedly intense pleasure. He grabbed her hips and thrust himself harder, watching her back arch, her perfect breasts rise, her head falling back on a moan. Passion roared through him, cleansing him of sleep and weakness, lifting him up as if on the winds of a storm. A storm that, like before, threatened to tear him loose and dash him into the seas.

He hadn't wanted to do this again.

With a rush, it all came back to him. Tarrys insinuating they needed to make love again. His denial. This was Tarrys's doing.

Dammit. *Dammit.*

If he could have pulled away from her at that moment, he would have, but he was powerless to do so. His body was lost in the feel of her, lost in the need.

He rolled, pulling her under him as he took over, taking her roughly. But by her expression, it became quickly apparent that his show of temper only excited her more. She met him thrust for thrust, her moans growing louder.

The exquisite pleasure on her delicate features made his heart ache. And made him only more desperate to put distance between them.

Damn her for pulling him back into this. For stealing his control.

Passion built in his blood, rising between them until he felt her release burst upon her, driving him to his own. With a roar of pleasure and frustration, he came, pumping his seed into her over and over again. When it was over, it was all he could do not to roll onto his back, holding her tight against his chest. Everything irrational inside him wanted to feel her heart pounding in time with his as he filled his senses with her sweet scent and felt her warm flesh against his.

Instead, he levered himself up and out of her, feeding on the anger in order to keep that unwanted need at bay.

"Don't ever do that to me again," he growled. Almost as soon as the words were out, he regretted his tone, hating the thought of hurting her.

As he grabbed his pants, Tarrys leaped to her feet, hands on her hips. To his surprise, temper flashed in her eyes.

"Do you notice anything odd about your clothes?" she snapped.

Wet. God, they were dripping. Everything about him was soaked. His brows drew down in confusion as he looked to her for explanation. He couldn't remember....

She picked up her gown and pulled it over her

head, not meeting his gaze. "You passed out, Charlie. Right into the water. When I pulled you out, your skin was more green than tan and I wasn't even sure you were breathing." She fastened the belt around her waist, then faced him, her mouth hard. "The only thing I could think to do was to share my power with you the only way I know how." Her mouth tightened even more, but her chin began to quiver as hot, angry eyes stared at him. "I'm sorry you find making love with me so disagreeable, but surely it's not worse than dying?"

Without waiting for his reply, she snatched up her quiver and bow and took off running in the direction they'd been traveling before the exhaustion overtook him.

Jesus. She thought he didn't want her. And he didn't, but…

Hell, of course he did. That was the whole damn problem.

His heart clenched, his anger crumbling. She'd been more loyal to him, and brought him more pleasure, than any woman he'd known.

The last thing he'd meant to do was hurt her. Wasn't that the reason he'd been trying to keep things from getting too hot and heavy between them? Because she'd end up getting hurt?

God, he'd made a mess of this.

With a shake of his head, he ran to catch up with her. As he moved, he was amazed all over again at his sudden and total recovery. Incredible.

He owed her an apology. Not only because he'd been unfair to her, but because making love to Tarrys was probably the only thing that was going to keep him alive.

God save his sanity.

When he caught up to her, she didn't meet his gaze but stared straight ahead as she continued to run, tears streaking her cheeks.

He felt like the world's biggest heel.

"Tarrys, I'm sorry. That was a hell of a way to thank you for saving my life."

As he kept pace beside her, he watched her, waiting for her to turn, forgiveness warming her violet eyes. Instead, she ignored him.

He'd really hurt her this time. But, seriously, she of all people should understand his getting ticked off at having sex forced on him. Except that wasn't it, was it? He remembered what she'd said. *I'm sorry you find making love with me so disagreeable.*

Hell. Surely she didn't believe that? And yet, why wouldn't she? How could she possibly know part of his problem was that he found making love to her entirely *too* agreeable? So much so that he felt as if he was losing himself every time he came inside her.

And that was something he refused to do... to lose himself, to care about someone so much that when they left him...

Hell, how could he ever expect her to understand him when he didn't understand himself?

"Tarrys." She continued to ignore him, so he pressed forward. "I don't find making love to you disagreeable. Not at all. Being with you has been the best sex I've ever had."

She looked at him and then turned away.

"The problem is, you love me. And I don't

love you." Now he was just digging himself a bigger hole. Somehow he had to make her understand. "It's not that I don't want to. It's that I *can't* love you. It's not in me."

He scrubbed his face with his hands. Love… the kind that made you dependent on another, that made you weak…wrecked lives. He'd seen it happen too many times. His dad's desertion had sent his mom spiraling down into depression and alcoholism, leaving his sons to fend for themselves at a tender age. At eleven years old he'd lost two parents, but learned a hard, if valuable, lesson—never let anyone matter so much that they destroy you when they leave. Harrison had failed to learn that lesson and was now divorced. Charlie refused to go down that path. He kept his relationships casual and short. Always.

"I don't want to lead you on, Tarrys. I don't want you to think I might fall in love with you someday. It's not fair to either one of us."

Her pace slowed as she looked at him with

genuine confusion. "What does love have to do with sex?"

He frowned. "Usually a lot."

The look she threw him told him clearly that she thought he was an idiot. "You're afraid my loving you makes me too weak to have sex with you?"

"No," he said with exasperation. "It's just…" Hell, he didn't even know what his point was anymore. Maybe it didn't have anything to do with her. It was him. He was the one in danger if he didn't pull away from her. Which was equally ridiculous.

"I'm not hurt that you don't love me, Charlie," Tarrys said softly. "I never expected you to. And since it makes you so uncomfortable, I won't say it again. But until we reach a carnasserie bush and the antidote for the trimor poisoning, I must share my power with you from time to time or you'll die." Temper snapped in her eyes. "But I will endeavor to quit loving you."

She was mocking him.

Or maybe she wasn't. His stomach fell away. Could she really quit caring that easily? Hell, why not? He'd certainly given her more than enough reason to.

But instead of being relieved at the thought, he felt like he'd been punched in the gut.

Nearly two weeks later, Charlie held Tarrys tight in his arms, her head tucked under his chin, her naked warmth covering the length of him as she lay atop him. He was still buried deep inside her and he knew it was time to get going again.

But his arms wouldn't budge even though a melancholy had invaded his mood as it always did when they had sex. If only he could hold on to the euphoria, the feeling of total rightness, that filled him whenever he sank into her. Every time, as he clung to the last threads of control, the euphoria drained away.

They were making love daily now. Tarrys had become a drug he craved ever since he'd quit fighting his need for her, accepting that for a reason he couldn't fathom, release inside her body kept the effects of the poison at bay. He needed to make love to her. He needed her, period.

Every day, he fell a little more under her spell. Every time he held her in his arms, he found it harder to let her go.

He stroked her hair and kissed the top of her head as he opened his eyes to the low ceiling of the tunnel. They'd left the ease of the caverns days ago. He had a recurring nightmare that these paths didn't actually lead anywhere. That they were part of a maze with no end that would leave them spiraling within the mountain forever. At moments like these, with Tarrys tight in his arms, he wasn't sure he cared. As long as they remained within the mountain, she'd never leave him.

The thought hit him from out of nowhere, jarring him unpleasantly, and he shoved it aside. "We need to get going."

Tarrys pulled back and looked down at him, her violet eyes glowing with fathomless intensity in the reddish light from the crystal. He lifted a hand and slid his thumb across her cheek. So beautiful. How was it possible to want her more each day than he had the day before?

Tarrys dipped her head to lay a kiss on his shoulder. Tenderness rose inside him until he thought it would swallow him whole, melding with the protectiveness that drove him every hour of every day. If he did nothing else, he would keep her safe.

She kissed his shoulder once more, then rose to her knees with a fluid grace that never ceased to impress him. As he rose from the cloak he'd laid out for them on the crystal floor, she pulled her torn and stained gown over her head. Even dressed in rags, she took his breath away.

He finished dressing and they set off again. They'd barely walked an hour when Tarrys whirled to stare at him.

"What's the matter?" he demanded.

"Do you smell that?"

He sniffed the air, smelling nothing but the sweet scent of the woman whose body he'd come to know as well as his own. "What do you smell?"

"Trees. We've found the way out of the mountain."

Their gazes met and locked, relief and dread arcing between them as they wondered what awaited them in the land beyond.

Chapter 18

Tarrys stared at Charlie's broad back with disbelief as he pushed her behind him. "What do you think you're doing?"

"Wrap your feet. If you're smelling trees, we're near an exit. We need to douse the light."

He was right, of course, and she quickly untied the strips of cloth she'd been wearing around her wrists for just such a situation. But that wasn't what was bothering her at the moment.

"Charlie, why would you shove me behind you? They know you're human. They'll come after you with arrows and knives, neither of which can hurt me. Let me go first."

"No. I'm leading from here on out."

Tarrys made a sound of exasperation. "Are you really going to start this again?"

He looked back at her, meeting her gaze, his jaw set. "I concede the wisdom of your words. But I'm not letting you take the brunt of the attack."

"That doesn't make any sense."

With a shrug, he turned back. "Doesn't matter."

"I'm virtually indestructible."

"A handy trick."

Tarrys stared at his back, frustration growing quickly into anger. "Charlie Rand, turn around, *now.*"

He glanced at her over his shoulder, meeting her gaze.

"Turn around," she said again. "I can't talk to you like this and I won't let you treat me like a slave, shuffling behind you with no say in what I'm forced to do."

The expression in his eyes sobered and he turned, kneeling so that he could straighten his back. She liked when he did this. It was the only time she could look down at him.

She took his beloved face in her hands. "You told me I was your partner. You know they can't hurt me. Yet you're trying to protect me anyway. *Don't be foolish.*"

He grabbed her hands and tugged her down onto her knees in front of him. "I'm not being protective. I'm being reasonable."

She gave him a disbelieving look.

"Okay, so I am being protective, but hear me out. If the Esri are out there, I'm dead. If they've caught up with me already, there's no hope for me."

"You could go back in the mountain."

"Only if you don't get captured. And for how long even then? You keep me going, but you can't heal me. I need the antidote, Tarrys. You know that. Without it, sooner or later, I'm going to die." He squeezed her hands. "I can't live without you. You *can* live without me. If they're out there, I want you to go back through the mountain. You can find your way to the gate and wait until the next full moon to return to D.C."

"Without you?"

His gaze melded with hers. "I want you safe. I want you free and happy, Tarrys. I don't want anything to happen to you."

"Nor I you."

"I'm not going to let them take you. As long as I'm alive, I'm going to keep you safe."

She stared at him, at the hard promise in his gaze, and felt her love for him deepen even more. No matter what happened, no matter that he didn't actually love her, the gift of his caring, of his knight's honor, would stay with her forever, tight beside the love she felt for him and the love she'd been showered with as a child. Sustenance during the long, cruel nights to come.

"So you're going to step out there and let them shoot you?" she asked.

His mouth compressed and he shook his head, a gleam in his eye. "Not at all. I'm not going down without one hell of a fight. If there's no one out there, I'll come back for you."

"No, Charlie. If safety had ever been my goal, I'd have stayed in D.C. I didn't risk everything to come with you only to hide now. You might leave the mine first, but I'll be right behind you."

Emotions chased one another across his face—frustration, anger, resignation. And, finally, acceptance.

"You're stubborn, you know that?"

"As are you."

The wry grin that broke over his face melted something deep inside her. "Yeah," he said. "I am. I think that's why I like you so much." He shook his head. "I'd really prefer to keep you safe."

Tarrys smiled, ruefully. "As I would you. I suppose neither of us will get their wish."

Charlie sighed. "I guess not. We'll do this together, then." He led the way, stopping a short while later. "There it is."

Tarrys peered around him. In the distance,

an opening in the crystal revealed the bright gold of the Esrian sky.

"No bushes," Charlie muttered. "If they're waiting for us, they're going to have a clean shot. Do you know this place? Do you know what the terrain is like out there?"

"Cliffs. Steep paths down the mountainside." Her eyes widened as she stared at him. "You can't run and leap, if that's what you were thinking."

"It was a thought. Okay." Rubbing his hands together, he eyed the cave mouth. "Let's do this."

He turned sideways, as much as he was able, and motioned her to do the same. Then, together, they eased their way toward the cave's mouth. With each careful step, Tarrys's heart pounded a little faster, a little harder until she thought it would fly from her chest.

Slavery she could survive. Even living without Charlie would be bearable as long as she knew he was back in his world and safe. But watching him die would destroy her. And if the Esri were out there, waiting, that's exactly what would happen.

Tarrys forced herself to breathe, pushing back the panic that crowded her lungs. She had to remain calm and focused to be of any help to him at all.

Charlie held up his hand, a silent command to stop while he peered out. The cave entrance was higher than the one on the other side of the mountain and he could almost stand erect.

The scent of fresh air wafted around her, welcoming and worrisome.

"Do you see anything?" she whispered.

He shook his head and took another step. Tarrys did the same, watching for any shadow, any sign of movement as she followed him closer to the outside. Slowly, the valley below became visible, shrouded in mist.

But still, she saw nothing move.

A couple feet from the entrance, Charlie stopped and hooked his arm around her shoulders, pulling her close. "Be careful."

"You, too."

As soon as he released her, she pulled her bow and grabbed an arrow, ready to counter-attack. Arrows wouldn't hurt an Esri, but one aimed just right might slow him down. Or make him miss his own shot. And that might be all it took to keep Charlie alive.

Charlie held up one finger. Two. As he held up three, he ducked low and lunged for the cave's mouth. Tarrys followed close behind. The brightness of the day hurt her eyes as she ran behind him, down the steep path, moving side to side as he'd told her to. But no arrows came sailing at them. No shouts.

A dozen yards down the path, Charlie ducked behind a boulder, his back to the red rock, and she joined him.

"Do you sense anyone?" he asked.

"No. Do you?"

"No."

"Then why are we hiding?"

He grinned at her. "It seemed like the smarter place to ask the question. But it does appear we've beaten them. How far to the Forest of Nightmares?"

"Several days' journey."

"We'll have to run," Charlie said.

"That'll be hard in the mists."

"You mean that fog in the valley? Won't it lift?"

"No. These are the mist lands. It's always like this."

"That might be good news if they couldn't sense us any better than we can sense them." But they could all follow his death mark. "How far do the mists extend?"

"They end a few miles from the Forest of Nightmares. We'll be in them almost the entire journey."

"Great," he muttered. "How are we supposed to find our way through them?"

Tarrys rose. "I'll lead you through."

Charlie stood beside her, peering around them in all directions. "Do you have some kind of internal compass or something?"

"I'm not sure what a compass is, but I know

the way. I've been through here before. And I understand my world."

"Then you're the official guide."

A short while later, they reached the bottom of the path and slipped into mists so thick she had to grip Charlie's hand to find him. She prayed she was leading him to safety. And not to his death.

"This stuff tastes like turpentine," Charlie muttered three days later, draining the canteen that contained the last of the carnasserie root infusion, the antidote to the black trimor's poison. They'd come upon one of the bushes their first day in the mist lands.

"It's saving your life. Give thanks, ungrateful one." Tarrys sat behind him on the stairs, kneading the tense muscles in his shoulders and neck.

The mists weren't helping his tension. He hated the feeling of not being able to see his enemies when he knew they could zero in on him without effort. The mists themselves were odd. They smelled all right, kind of like a musty sea spray, but they had a wet, cloying feel that clung to his skin yet didn't actually make his hair or clothing damp.

They swirled now through the ruins of some kind of structure he and Tarrys had literally stumbled upon a short while ago.

"Ungrateful, huh? You didn't have to drink this swill."

"And now neither will you. This is the last of it."

"That's what you said yesterday," he muttered. Though he teased her, traveling virtually blind for three days was making him as edgy as a cat on a high wire. He'd ended up with a blasting headache yesterday. Tarrys had offered to try to ease some of the tension in his shoulders to keep that from happening again.

"Yes, well, I didn't know I'd find another bush so soon. An extra dose won't hurt you. Now I'm sure you're completely cured." Tarrys placed a soft kiss on his cheek, sending his protective instincts skyrocketing again. He hated putting her in danger, but he had to admit, he'd never have made it without her.

If Tarrys was right, they should be close to the forest by now. But how they'd ever find it in this soup, he couldn't begin to guess. All he could do was follow her and hope she knew where she was going. And pray he heard the Esri before they attacked.

"I was probably cured three bushes ago."

Tarrys laughed softly. "You are such a complainer."

Affection surged through him and he flipped her over his shoulder and onto his lap. "Who are you calling a complainer?" He tried to look angry, but couldn't. Every time she spoke, every time she touched him, she eased something deep inside him. Sliding his fingers into her thick, soft hair, he kissed her deeply because he had to, because he needed to ground himself in her taste and the feel of her in his arms.

He hadn't made love to her since they left the mines, afraid to let his guard down like that when they were so vulnerable. But already he was suffering from withdrawal. He might not need her to stay alive any longer, thanks to the carnasserie root, but he was beginning to realize he needed her in other ways, ways he didn't fully comprehend.

With another kiss, he set her on her feet. "You tempt me, little one." Tempted him. Pleased him. Healed him.

As he filled his water flasks from the pond Tarrys had called, his gaze fell on the beautifully carved stone pillars that lay at broken angles like a child's discarded blocks.

"What was this place?" he asked.

"I'm not sure. There are a number of ruins similar to this scattered throughout the mist lands. My old master used to pass this way every few years. I've always assumed this was an old Esrian court before the mists made living here unpleasant. But I don't know."

"You came through here with Baleris?"

"No. Baleris was my third master. My first was the captain of the crystal mines. When I came into my virgin's power, he sold me. He could have taken it himself, but a virgin has much value in this world, so he sold me for a great deal of money to a passing nobleman. Not Baleris."

"He raped you."

"He took my virgin's power, yes, but he made me want him first." She wrapped her arms around her knees. "That master was brutal in other ways. He had a dozen Marceils, but forbade us from touching one another or speaking at all. For nearly forty years, no words left my mouth."

He stared at her. *"None?"*

She shrugged. "An Esri's control over his slaves is complete. But we managed to communicate with one another without words."

Forty years. "The son of a bitch." How could anyone do such a thing to another?

"That wasn't the worst of it," she said softly.

Charlie watched her, not liking the glimmer of misery he saw in her eyes. "Tell me. If you want to."

She looked away. "It's unpleasant, Charlie. I shouldn't have brought it up."

Reaching for her, he slid his hand over the back of her head. "It's part of your past, part of who you are. If you can bear to tell it, I can bear to listen."

The eyes she turned to him fastened on him as if seeking the truth of his words. Slowly she turned away and began to speak.

"He enjoyed bringing the females into a frenzy of needing, painful needing. Then he left us like that."

He frowned, remembering too well her desperation for penetration when they first reached the mines.

"I learned to use other things to bring myself relief, though sometimes he'd tie me so I couldn't even do that. One time he left me like that for four days."

Charlie swore. "A real bastard."

"A few years ago, he was called back to court and he sold me to the drifter, Baleris. Baleris already had one slave, Yuillin. But he wanted a female."

Charlie's gut tightened, sick at the thought of the abuse she'd described, and certain she'd touched on only the tip of the iceberg. She'd been tortured. But he knew that. He'd known it on some level since he first met her and realized she'd been a slave to these creatures. But he hadn't really understood. Not until he'd seen the slave forced to stab himself, then watched Tarrys in so much misery she would have welcomed rape.

He took her hand and rubbed his thumb over her silken skin. "I can't imagine...." He shook his head, unable to find the words. "I always thought Baleris had to have been the worst, but his predecessor sounds as bad."

"No, Baleris was the worst. Baleris enjoyed inflicting pain."

With his free hand, he reached out and tucked her hair behind her ear. "I'm sorry for all you've endured. I wish I could make it all go away."

She smiled softly and met his gaze. "You have. Every time you touch me, every time you kiss me, every time you treat me as an equal, you give me strength and sweep away a little more of the past. I thank you, Charlie Rand."

He didn't know what to say to that, so he kissed her, tasting her Mona Lisa smile. How had she ever endured what she had? How was he ever going to walk away from her when they got home? When it was time for him to go back to his life?

Keep her, a voice whispered deep in his mind. *Impossible,* his heart replied. His path through life was only wide enough for one.

Less than an hour later, they crested a small rise and walked out of the mist as cleanly as if they'd walked through a door into the bright golden light of midday. The ground rolled, familiar blue dotted with shrubs and bushes. And no sign of Esri. Thank God.

In the distance stood a forest as dark and foreboding as its name.

The Forest of Nightmares.

"That's it, isn't it?"

"Yes."

On the surface, the trees didn't seem that close together. Logically, the forest shouldn't be that dark. But no light penetrated. None. In the bright day, those woods were dark as a moonless night. Scary as sin and, ironically, his only chance of survival. From what Tarrys had told him, no Esri would willingly enter that place.

"Let's go." He took off at a run, careful to keep his strides in sync with Tarrys's as he watched for sign of Esri. "I don't suppose you have a plan for finding the princess and getting us out of there."

Tarrys glanced at him. "I don't. This was your mission, remember."

"The mission was only to reach the Forest of Nightmares and rescue the princess. The details of the rescue have always been a little fuzzy." Then again, he was a pro at improvising. Up until now, he'd only been concerned with reaching the forest.

And they weren't there yet.

"How close are we to the full moon?" Tarrys asked.

"If my watch has been keeping the correct time, it's tomorrow night." And this day was already half done.

"We don't have much time left. If we don't get Princess Ilaria out by tomorrow night, we'll have to stay another month."

"Then we'll get her out." Charlie glanced at her. "If what Kade heard is true, one of the twelve gates lies within the forest. Will you be able to find it?"

Tarrys shook her head. "Not unless I stumble upon it when it's open. I can't see the gates and can only sense them when I'm virtually on top of them. Princess Ilaria may know where it is."

"So you won't even know when it opens?"

"Unless things have changed now that all twelve are open, no."

Charlie snorted. He'd thought reaching the forest would be the hard part. He was beginning to realize that the real challenge still lay ahead.

The first mile passed easily. But just as they crossed the halfway point between the mist and the forest, an odd rumbling began to vibrate beneath his feet.

"Do you feel that?" he asked Tarrys.

Her wide-eyed stare swung to him. "*Horses. Royal Guards!*"

"Damn!"

Chapter 19

Charlie ran, Tarrys at his side, pounding across the grass-dotted blue terrain, toward the spookiest sight he'd ever seen—the utter blackness of the Forest of Nightmares.

The closer they drew to the dark wood, the more every instinct he possessed yelled at him to go back, as if the ghosts of those who'd died there were flying around him, screaming at him, flaying him with their silent fear.

But the pounding of the Esri horses had been growing steadily louder.

Beside him, Tarrys ran, her hair whipping back, her face a mask of concentration and determination. If she was terrified, and she had to be, she didn't show it. His admiration for her tripled. Her body might be small and delicate-looking, but there was nothing delicate about the size of her heart or the strength of her spirit. He couldn't have asked for a better companion.

He glanced at Tarrys. "Are these horses like I think of horses, or another strange Esri creature?

"They're from your world," she told him breathlessly.

He threw her a confused glance. "My world? Fifteen centuries ago?"

"Their sires were. Humans can't breed here. The Esri tried often enough. But your horses can."

"Damn. I should have brought my gun."

"You would kill a horse?"

"I'll kill anything I have to in order to keep us alive and unenslaved. An arrow between the eyes will do it, Tarrys. You can't be soft."

She threw him a look of such affront it made him smile. "I'm not soft."

"You're not, I agree. There's no one I'd rather have by my side right now."

Her expression turned skeptical.

"I mean it."

A look of wonder warmed her eyes. "Truly?"

He nodded once. "Truly."

As she turned to face forward, he caught a glimpse of her smile and he thought his affection for her might swallow him whole.

They were in a shallow valley, which hid them from their pursuers for now. Or rather, hid their pursuers from them. The Esri knew exactly where he was. He thought he could make out the distinct sound of four animals. Maybe five.

"How large is the king's stable?"

"I've heard there are five."

"Just five? *In all of Esria?*"

"They breed here, but not easily."

"Then it sounds like they've sent them all. They'll be coming from the right. We should be able to see them when we crest this ridge coming up." They were still close to a mile from the forest's edge. What he wouldn't give for a car about now. Or a tank.

Never breaking stride, Tarrys pulled her bow off her shoulder, grabbed an arrow and cocked it. His tiny dancer had turned into Robin Hood. Robin Hood in a Friar Tuck robe. How she ran in that thing was beyond him, but she didn't seem to be tiring any more than he was. Then again, fear was a powerful energizer. For both of them.

As they crested the hill, the riders appeared in the distance, five men, white as ghosts, dressed in the requisite silver tunics, black pants and cloaks of the Royal Guard. At the rate they were traveling, the Esri would be on them long before they reached the woods.

"If they take me down, Tarrys, keep moving. You can hide out in the forest until they're gone."

The look she threw him was pure determination coated with acceptance and unhappiness. "I'll find the princess. Your mission will become mine." Her eyes flashed. "But don't you dare give up, yet."

He grinned at her. "Not a chance."

As the Esri neared, he caught his first good look at their horses. My God. Their heads were misshapen, their snouts too short and slanted upward, and they didn't have a bit of hair. No manes, no tail except a bony-looking stump. One of the creatures appeared to be jet-black, but the rest all had flesh of a pinkish-white. They were, without a doubt, the ugliest animals he'd ever seen.

"Those things are *not* horses," he muttered. Horselike creatures from some horror story, maybe. "Shoot them, Tarrys. Take them out of their misery."

She threw him a quick look of amusement. "I'd rather take the Esri out of theirs." As she spoke, she started firing arrow after arrow. True to her word, he watched her arrows pierce the eyes of the Esri. Shouts of pain echoed over the field as three of the five lost their seats and crashed to the ground, their mounts scattering.

"Nice shots!" Charlie crowed.

But the other two guards kept their heads and their seats. As if choreographed, the pair reached up and pulled the arrows out of their eyes at almost the same moment, tossing them aside.

Tarrys released another volley, all three going through the face of one man, knocking him to the ground.

"Nice job."

Tarrys nodded, but there was no triumph in her expression. "I'm out of arrows."

Hell. The fallen guards were already on their feet, running toward the forest to cut them off. Keeping immortals down was an impossible task, no matter how many arrows you had.

Interestingly, each of the guards carried a bow and quiver of his own.

"They're not shooting at us. Maybe they don't realize I'm human."

"Perhaps the king has ordered you brought back alive."

Her words chilled him. As much as he didn't

want to die, it beat the hell out of being en-slaved or even tortured to death.

"We've got to reach that forest," he muttered.

"I agree."

But the lone Esri still on horseback was bear-ing down on them fast, his white hair flying out behind him like a second cloak. Neon-blue eyes gleamed with malice and purpose while beneath him the pale hairless *thing* that should have been a horse pulled lips back to reveal daggerlike teeth. *Jesus.* Straight out of a horror flick. Both of them. And they were closing on them fast.

"Tarrys, wait here!" Charlie barked. "I have a plan."

"To get trampled?" she asked even as she did as he demanded.

Damn, but she was getting a smart little mouth on her. If their situation hadn't been so dire, he might have smiled. If he could just pull off a miracle, he might yet live to taste that mouth again.

Charlie continued a few more yards, then

slowed to a stop, his gaze locking with the Esri's. In those brilliant blue eyes he saw victory. A victory he intended to steal. As the distance closed between them, he braced for impact. A split second before the horse ran him down, Charlie dove, grabbing the hairless creature around the neck. Levering himself up, he rammed his feet into the Esri's side, knocking him off the animal and onto the ground as Charlie swung onto the horse's back.

Righting himself on the slippery, sweaty animal's back was trickier than he'd expected, but he managed the feat, clenching his thighs and grabbing the reins to steady himself. As the furious Esri lunged for him, two arrows sailed through the guard's eye sockets. The Esri cried out, stumbling back.

Charlie didn't know where Tarrys had found the arrows, and didn't care. He swung his mount toward her, grabbed her hand and hauled her up behind him.

"Hold on," he shouted, and urged the animal forward. The Esri on foot didn't stand a chance of catching them, but one had reclaimed his horse and was now giving chase. He couldn't be certain the white bastards wouldn't follow them into the forest. In fact, he was almost certain they would. From what Kade had said, the Esri ruler, King Rith, did not accept failure. If he'd told them to kill or capture Charlie, they weren't going to give up until they had.

All he could hope was that whatever lay in that dark wood gave the Esri as much trouble as it was bound to give them.

They were nearly to the forest when the horse pulled up suddenly.

"What's the matter?" Tarrys asked.

Charlie tried to urge the animal forward, but the creature sidestepped, backing away. "He's as spooked by that place as I am. He's not going in. We're going to have to run for it."

An arrow sailed by them, winging the horse's ear.

"Jump!"

As the horse reared, Charlie dove off, rolling to his feet. Tarrys sprinted past him, picking up the arrows as they hit the ground without ever breaking stride. He took off after her, arrows continuing to whiz past him. Though the Esri clearly lacked Tarrys's talent with the bow, he doubted they'd be missing him so completely if they weren't determined to keep him alive. Intentional wounding took a lot more skill than shooting to kill.

Tarrys, several strides ahead of him, reached the woods first, disappearing as cleanly as if she'd walked through the Dupont Circle Fountain's gate. For an instant, his heart stopped beating.

His instincts screamed at him to slow down. He had no idea what he was racing into!

An arrow flew past so close he felt the feathers in his hair, erasing his hesitation. He dove into the wall of darkness, praying there was nothing worse waiting for him on the other side.

The darkness parted for him as it had for Tarrys. A blast of cold, fear-ridden air hit him a split second before he ran into her, knocking them both off their feet. Charlie grabbed her and rolled, taking the brunt of the fall, watching as two more arrows sailed over his head.

"You okay?" he asked her, holding her tight against him, her hair brushing his suddenly frigid cheek.

"Yes."

"Good. We've got to keep moving. But stay low." He released her and crouched as he followed her deeper into a forest straight out of a Halloween horror movie. Dark mists swirled, not thick like in the mist lands, but alive and menacing. The trees themselves were black, as if the entire forest had burned and was waiting only for the touch of a finger to disintegrate into ash.

With each step, the air turned colder, more menacing, as if even it were alive.

His pulse raced, his throat tightening, but his mind held strong, refusing to fold. The fear wasn't real. He knew manipulation when he saw it and this was a first-class job.

"Do you feel it?" he asked Tarrys, frustrated

to hear his teeth chattering. Unfortunately, unlike at home, this place seemed able to force the emotions on him even when his mind rebelled.

"Feel what?" She darted from one place to the next, retrieving the arrows the Esri shot.

Another flew past them several feet away.

"The cold. The fear."

Her head snapped to his, her eyes narrowed. "No. The temperature hasn't changed."

Charlie nodded. "I figured it wasn't real." Now if he could only figure out how to defend himself against that crawling mist and shut down its effect on him because, *damn,* he was starting to shake.

Tarrys's gaze shifted behind him, her eyes widening. "Esri. They've followed us."

Charlie grabbed her and pulled her behind the nearest tree, then eased out to look…and nearly took an arrow in the face. He reared back just as the projectile flew past to land in a tree behind him.

His gaze met the Esri's. The promise of death flashed in the Royal Guard's eyes.

Charlie cupped the back of Tarrys's head, needing the feel of her solid warmth. "We've got to keep moving or we're going to be captured."

"I need his arrows."

"He'll shoot you."

She met his gaze. "Good. Then I won't have to hunt for them."

His cool warrior's mind shoved down the fear swirling through his head. Tarrys was indestructible. They couldn't hurt her as long as they didn't catch her.

"Get your arrows," he said. Then he turned into himself, waging war with the forces battling his mind. He'd long ago learned to capture the adrenaline of gut-ripping fear and turn it into energy. The trick was to separate his body from his mind. Compartmentalization in its purest form.

Never had he needed it so completely.

"Tell me if they're coming," he told Tarrys,

then closed his eyes and took five deep breaths as he always did to corral his focus at the start of a dangerous op. Little by little, for another count of five, he consciously allowed the cold to wash through him as he siphoned the adrenaline that pounded through his veins. But as he tried to shut off the useful, if unwanted, emotion, it turned on him, terror leaping into his throat.

He couldn't shut it off. His vision began to spin in a whirl of chaos, screams tearing apart his ears.

"Tarrys!" He couldn't see her. Couldn't see anything! Screams. Her screams. She needed him.

Something clamped around his wrist. Soft. Warm.

"Charlie, I'm right here."

His vision cleared instantly. Inside his mind, he slammed down a mental wall, shutting off the forest's evil, breaking its hold.

He breathed air into his lungs, air that suddenly tasted warm again. But that particular battle wasn't over. He could still see the dark mists swirling around him. Just the thought of being overcome again sent a frigid draft brushing against his cheeks and he got the distinct feeling that the forest laughed at him, laughed at his temerity in thinking he could possibly defend himself against its attack.

The chill that went through him was all too real.

He turned to Tarrys. "Where's the Esri?"

"Right where he was a moment ago, but he's no longer shooting at us. He's not moving."

Charlie peered around the tree. Sure enough, the guard was staring at nothing, his eyes huge. Charlie nearly smiled. Misery loved company.

"Let's get going before the others join him." He glanced at the three arrows clutched in Tarrys's hand. "Did you get what you needed?"

"The ones close by."

Charlie ushered her in front of him as they dodged from tree to tree, careful not to touch the ones with thorns. They'd made little progress when another flurry of arrows sailed past them, one catching in his cloak. Another caught Tarrys in the back of her shoulder.

He grabbed her when she would have stumbled, and pulled her behind the closest tree. Pain lanced her features.

"Tell me what to do."

"Don't break it! I need the arrow."

Cringing against the pain he knew he was going to cause her, he grabbed the shaft and yanked it free of her tender flesh, releasing a fresh bloom of blood to mark her ragged gown. He held her tight as she sagged against him, absorbing her shudders as the shock roared through her system. As her body healed.

Charlie glanced back, ready to pick her up and run if the Esri were getting too close. But three of the four who were now inside the forest had turned and were fleeing the other way, leaving the forest as cleanly as they'd entered. Only one remained, but he posed no threat at the moment because he was staring with wide, terrified eyes at something that was invisible to Charlie.

The forest seemed to be really doing a number on the Royal Guard, far worse than on him or Tarrys. Were they stronger, or had the forest yet to turn its full power on them? He supposed they'd know soon enough.

"I'm healed," Tarrys said against his chest.

Charlie loosened his tight grip on her and peered down into her face.

"I wish you could teach me how to do that."

"It's one of the advantages of being Marceil." Her eyes shadowed. "Perhaps the only advantage."

He dropped a kiss on her hair. "The forest has run off the Esri. At least for now. Let's get going."

"What do you mean, *the forest?*"

Charlie looked back as the last of the Esri fled. "You still don't feel that cold black mist?"

"No." She looked at him with confusion. "It's just a forest, Charlie."

"If you say so." He grabbed her hand. It was time to find Princess Ilaria and start working on a plan to free her. But he'd taken only a few steps when movement made him freeze. Half a dozen Esri stepped out from behind trees, surrounding him, bows raised, arrows pointed at his heart.

No fear clouded the eyes of this group. The only thing gleaming from those brightly colored depths was death.

His.

Chapter 20

Charlie yanked Tarrys behind him. "Run!"

"Why?"

Why? "They'll catch you."

"Who will?"

Even as his heart hammered against his ribs, his logical mind pushed its way to the fore, shoving back his emotions. "I see six Esri, all aiming arrows at me."

"I don't see anyone."

"Crap." The damned forest again. The nearest Esri's mouth lifted into a smirk, but he didn't disappear.

And Charlie's pulse wouldn't calm, not with six arrows aimed at him.

Tarrys squeezed his hand. "Are they still there?"

"Oh yeah. Still there and laughing at me. It's this damned woods. No wonder they say no one leaves this place with their mind intact. How am I supposed to know what's real and what's not?"

"Ask me."

He tore his gaze from the Esri in front of him and glanced at her. "Ask you?"

"I'm not seeing anything weird. If you see it and I don't, it's probably not there. And vice versa."

Charlie's gaze snapped back, scanning the Esri one by one, returning to the one in front of him. He was sure he'd never seen the guy before. So the creature hadn't come from any memory.

He met the Esri's gaze. "Can you hear me?"

The Esri didn't respond. Nor did his expression change to indicate he'd heard Charlie's question.

Charlie squeezed Tarrys's hand. "Stay here. I

need to check this out for myself." He released her and stepped forward, his gaze locked on the Esri's. He moved left and the Esri's aim moved, keeping him in his sights.

He could feel the pulse thrumming through his body, the adrenaline raging as he walked toward an enemy who, if he released a real arrow, would kill him in an instant. An enemy who, according to Tarrys, wasn't even there. He marveled at how much he'd come to trust her.

Slowly, he closed the distance between them. "You're not there, you son of a bitch," he said quietly, not stopping until the bow and arrow were within reach of his hand. In one swift motion, he grabbed for the bow, intending to shove it up and away from him. But his hand touched nothing.

The Esri wasn't there.

Charlie closed his eyes, ignoring his sight, and forced himself to "see" with his other senses as he'd been trained to do. Shutting out his vision, he heard Tarrys breathing behind him. And knew, *knew,* they were alone. But when he opened his eyes, the bastards were staring at him.

Charlie strode forward, right through the closest Esri. Right through nothing.

He turned back to Tarrys and came nose to nose with the same damned guard. With a growl, he stepped around him this time and motioned for Tarrys.

"Do you still see the Esri?" she asked, hurrying over to him.

"Clear as day. But I can walk right through them." When she reached him, he hooked his arm around her shoulders and pulled her close. "I'm glad you're not seeing them. If we both start seeing them, we're in trouble." Because if there was one thing Kade had assured him, Esri lived in these woods. Princess Ilaria and her jailers had been here for more than three hundred years. "How have Ilaria and her guards survived this for centuries?"

Tarrys frowned. "I don't know. Maybe they're like me and not affected by it."

"If that's the case, I'm in trouble."

"If that's *not* the case and they're all mentally crippled, Princess Ilaria may be worthless to you."

Charlie grunted. "So either Ilaria's damaged goods or I'm dead. Nice choice."

"There may be another explanation for how Ilaria's lived in these woods all this time." He looked at her expectantly, but she just shrugged. "I don't know what it is. I'm just saying there might be another explanation."

"We can hope." He released her shoulders and took her hand. "Let's go find her."

The dark mists continued to swirl through the black trees, but the cold no longer bothered him. He looked at his watch. It was late in the day, the day before the full moon, if time passed the same here as it did at home. A little over a day to find Ilaria and free her. Which might be plenty of time. Or might be hopelessly too little.

He glanced back to find his Esri nightmare following him, their arrows aimed at his back, smirks upon their mouths. How would he possibly hold on to his sanity if he had to deal with this 24/7 for another month? Heaven help him. But his gaze went to Tarrys and a part of him wanted to do just that. Stay here, lost in this fantasy world with her by his side for a little longer.

"Look at the birds," Tarrys murmured.

Charlie followed her gaze to where dozens of tiny birds, like brightly colored hummingbirds, lined the branches of the dead trees, their trilling songs somehow pleasing. But a flash of black close to the ground had him turning rigid. A second flash confirmed he hadn't imagined the first glimpse of a creature that filled him with more dread than the Esri. A creature with black fur and three white horns.

"Black trimors. Two of them."

Tarrys cocked an arrow. "Where?"

The two reappeared, briefly, along with three others pacing behind them. "Crap. They're all around us."

"Charlie, I don't see anything."

"They're invisible most of the time."

"They're probably just visions."

"Do you want to take that chance? Besides, I can hear them growling. Can't you hear that?"

"No. I only hear the birds."

He groaned. "How am I supposed to be able to tell, then?"

One was fully visible now, eyeing him like prey. Slowly, he pulled his knife. If the creature disappeared, it wouldn't do anything. But if it would just stay whole…

Charlie flung the knife through the fully corporeal beast. The knife sailed right through.

"Dammit."

"I don't see them, Charlie, and I would if they were here."

How could his eyes and ears deceive him so thoroughly? Out of his left peripheral vision, he saw one leap for him. Instinctively, he lifted his arm in front of his face while he pulled his second knife. He stabbed the beast at the moment it should have attached itself to his arm. And thrust through nothing but air.

Adrenaline poured through his body, making his heart pound.

"It attacked you?" Tarrys asked.

He scowled at her. "No, I was playacting," he said with ill-concealed sarcasm. Her grin eased some of the enormous tension riding him. He shook his head. "No wonder the Esri turned and ran."

The trimors were all visible now, five of them pacing, ready to spring. He braced himself as a different trimor attacked, lifting his arm because he had to, but not bothering with his knife this time. He was going to have a bloody heart attack if this kept up much longer. Forcing himself to ignore the beasts, he continued on, walking within inches of one of the trimor's horns.

He glanced at Tarrys. "Why aren't the visions bothering you?"

"I don't know. Maybe I'll start seeing them later." She gasped. "Charlie. Unicorns!"

He followed her gaze, certain this had to be the first of her visions because, hell, there was no such thing as a unicorn. Except there was definitely something down the path. Three somethings, shaggy blue ponies with white manes and tails. Protruding from the middle of each forehead was a blue-tipped white horn.

"*That's* a unicorn?"

"Of course. They're wonderful eating."

He gaped at her. "You eat *unicorns?*"

She cocked her head. "Do you have unicorns in your realm?"

He laughed, then realized she was serious. Of course, she was serious. She was a brownie in an enchanted forest deep in fairyland who liked to eat unicorns. Any minute now he was going to wake up in the psych ward of some military hospital with a pretty doctor shaking her head at him, ordering him locked away in a padded room for the rest of his life.

"Unicorns aren't real," he told her. "In my world, they're not real. They're legends. Mythical, magical beasts."

Tarrys smiled gently. "These are quite real, quite common, and not magical at all."

"Those horns look wicked." They were nearly as long as his forearm.

"They use them to dig for grubs."

Grubs. In blue dirt. Hence the blue tips. "You're shooting the myth to hell, you know."

Her grin widened and she swung away as she watched the beasts. "They're usually very timid. I'm surprised they're letting us get so close." But as they continued toward the blue beasts, the unicorns raised their heads and began to trot toward them.

Charlie grabbed Tarrys's shoulder. "Get back."

But his concern was met with amusement. "Charlie, they're harmless. And they can't hurt me even if they wanted to." She eased out from beneath his protective hand and met the creatures, who greeted her as if they were favored pets. Amazingly, though they rubbed their heads against her hips, their horns never touched her.

The flock of tiny birds joined them, fluttering about Tarrys's head, landing on the backs of the unicorns, singing a melodious tune that sounded ridiculously...happy.

Tarrys's laughter rang through the forest and Charlie stared at her. It was like dropping into the middle of a Disney movie. Cinderella in her rags, petting unicorns while birds danced and sang around her head. If these were her nightmares, there was something seriously wrong with this girl. Except this wasn't a vision. It was a hundred percent, absurdly real.

Another black trimor leaped at him, and he only flinched, no longer bothering to protect himself from the animal that wasn't there.

Tarrys turned to him, her eyes sparkling like jewels. Her laughter wove through him, easing his tension, warming him. Filling him with a joy of his own. "Come here, Charlie. You've got to see them. Aren't they beautiful?"

Beautiful, yes. Not the ponies, but Tarrys. Achingly so.

He moved slowly toward her, not wanting to scare off her new friends. The unicorns eyed him cautiously, but didn't move away as he joined her. She looked up at him, a poignant mist in her eyes. "They like me."

He slid his hand into her hair. "How could they not?" She was so perfect, so precious. His head dipped before he knew what he was doing. The touch of her lips against his swept him away. Her mouth moved under his, her tongue welcoming his own as her arms went tightly around him.

So precious.

He hadn't meant to kiss her, certainly hadn't meant to get lost in the taste of her again, but he had little control where she was concerned. He needed her. Man, how he needed her. Slowly he pulled away to discover even more birds singing from the trees.

"This forest loves you," he muttered, then looked back down at her, tumbling into violet depths as deep as the sea. And with a sudden, haunting certainty, he knew the forest wasn't the only one. God, he didn't want to love her. Yet how could he not? How could anyone not?

He pulled back and released her, shaken. Another trimor leaped for him and he flung up an arm. Movement in the distance caught his eye. An eighteen-wheeler was now racing toward him. In Esria. Touching none of the trees. Glancing behind him, he saw the contingent of Esri still aiming at him, black trimors prowling between them.

"This forest hates me."

Tarrys took his hand. "Don't see them, Charlie. They're not there."

And suddenly they weren't. Charlie stared, chilled by the suddenness of the transformation. Between one instant and the next, the Esri and trimors disappeared, the dark mists vanished and golden daylight filtered into the woods between the colorful leaves of healthy trees.

Even the truck had vanished, though...really? A truck? His gaze swung to Tarrys. "How'd you do that?"

"Do what?"

"You made them disappear."

"I did?"

"Your power's growing."

She crinkled her brow. "I don't feel any different. But something's definitely happening here." A soft confusion lit her eyes. "I belong here, somehow."

Charlie looked at the unicorns and the birds. "Yeah. You could say that. Yet you say you've never been here before."

"I haven't. I've seen the forest from the distance, but I've never been inside."

He tugged on her hand. "We need to keep going if we're going to find the princess and figure out how to spring her by tomorrow night."

As they walked, the unicorns followed the birds trilling overhead. They'd gone from horror show to Disney movie in a matter of minutes and he had a feeling the day's entertainment wasn't over. When Tarrys's hand spasmed around his, he knew he was right.

"What's the matter?"

"I see Marceils. With hair," she said, her

voice filled with wonder. But her eyes were facing down and unfocused.

Charlie looked around to make sure, but saw only unicorns, birds, and half a dozen of the neon-green chipmunks that had joined the procession.

"There isn't anyone here, Tarrys. Whatever you're seeing isn't real."

"It's real," she murmured. "What I'm seeing isn't happening now, but it's real. And I'm getting answers."

Chapter 21

Tarrys could feel Charlie's hand in hers and knew he stood beside her, holding her against him, but her senses were elsewhere. Even though they were standing deep in the Forest of Nightmares, she sensed that they'd stumbled upon another time. Another era.

In front of her, beneath a tall thornewood tree, stood two people, a man and a woman, with eyes only for one another. Neither was as tall as Tarrys, but the man was thickly muscled and handsome with eyes as blue as the human sky. The woman was slender, her eyes as violet as Tarrys's own. Both had rich brown hair, his brushing his shoulders, hers in a straight fall to her waist, intertwined with golden silk ribbons.

The man took the woman in his arms, his eyes filled with love, his face aglow with happiness, then kissed her tenderly, passionately. As they kissed, flowers rose from the earth around their feet, blooming in a profusion of pink and yellow and blue.

When he finally pulled back, the woman looked down at the flowers, then up into her man's face and laughed with a joy so pure it brought tears to Tarrys's eyes.

"You are my one mate," the man said, his voice low and rich with love. "As I told you."

The woman kissed his mouth. "Aye. And you mine."

They kissed again and the man's hands slid up to cover one of the woman's small breasts. "I don't know if I can wait to mate with you."

The woman's mouth turned up. "Our joining ceremony is only seven nights away. Then we'll be together fully and always."

But the joy between them shattered with a shout.

"*The Esri!*" *Another woman with hair more red than brown crashed through the woods toward them.* "*They're in the forest.*"

The couple gaped at each other, horror dawning in their expressions. "*But that's impossible!*"

"*I feared this would happen,*" *said the auburn-haired woman, as the three began to run.* "*We're strong, but the Esri are stronger. The villages are all destroyed, the people enslaved. Only the temple village remains. I've always feared they would come for us.*"

"*But the forest magic is strong,*" *said the first woman, her straight hair flying out behind her.* "*I've strengthened it myself.*"

"*Three Esri found a way through undetected. I don't know how, but it doesn't matter now.*" *Tears were beginning to stream down her face.* "*All is lost.*"

"*No,*" *the man said, his voice strong and emphatic.* "*We'll fight them. They'll not beat us.*

How can they possibly win against the power of our priestesses?" But the words were barely out of his mouth when an arrow struck him in the leg, sending him crashing to the ground.

"No!" his love cried, falling to her knees beside him.

"Run!" He grabbed her hand. "Run to the temple. Save yourself and your sisters. If you fall, if our priestesses fall, all is truly lost."

"I love you," she whispered, tears in her eyes.

"And I you. For always. Now go!"

The two women ran. The man worked the arrow from his calf. But as he rose, another arrow pierced his neck and his thigh. A tall, white Esri ran out of the shelter of the trees, fell on him and cut off his hair.

"Rise, slave," the Esri commanded, and the blue-eyed Marceil did as he was told. "Deliver me to your priestesses."

Slowly, Tarrys became aware of Charlie holding her tight against him, stroking her hair. She was shaking, not with fear or cold, but with the shock of sudden knowledge, sudden under-standing. And shadows of things to come.

"It's okay, Tarrys. There's nothing here but me and the unicorns. And the birds. And a few chipmunks. And whatever the heck the pink turtle things are."

Tarrys looked up at him, the gentle affection in his gaze washing away the cold. "The Mar-ceils created the magic that lives in this forest. The forest protected the last of the unenslaved Marceils against the Esri."

Charlie glanced at the unicorns. "No wonder the forest and everything in it seems to love you."

Her eyes widened. "Maybe that's why I could order you to stop seeing the nightmares and you did. If the Marceils created the defense, they must have had a way to allow friends through."

"You think they had friends among the Esri?"

She thought of the terror she'd witnessed in that vision. "Probably not." But she'd been deeply moved by what she saw. "I've always thought of mine as a slave race. I knew we hadn't always been so, but no Marceils remember that time and none were allowed by their Esri masters to share it with their children. The past was lost to us. All we knew was slavery and weakness."

Charlie slid his hand beneath her hair, cupping the back of her neck. "You're not weak."

"I was. Until my hair was allowed to grow."

He shook his head, his gray-green eyes warm and serious despite the half smile. "No. You've never been weak. You were born a fighter. Even decades of slavery didn't break you. Baleris was a powerful son of a bitch, yet you thwarted him. Without your help, we never would have defeated him." His thumb stroked her jaw, sending warmth flowing through her. "You've never been weak." He grimaced. "If you want to talk about weak, look at the zombies humans become when they're enslaved by the Esri."

"That's not weak, it's enchanted."

"Exactly. Marceils were never weak, just overpowered in an unfair fight. We do have a lot in common, don't we?" Laughter crinkled his eyes and made her chest tight with longing. For his kiss. For his love. But mostly, for his safe return to his world where his laughter would continue for years to come. And if she could go back with him, her happiness would be complete. Even if she rarely saw him again. The only thing that mattered was getting him safely home and helping him save his world.

"Did that vision tell you anything else?"

She nodded. "A millennia and a half ago, during the Esri's enslavement of the Marceilian race, the forest acted as the defense for the temple village. But the Esri found a way to breach it."

"So at the center of the woods is a village. Probably where they're keeping Ilaria."

"Yes."

"Then that's where we have to go."

Chapter 22

"How deep is this forest?" Charlie muttered. They'd walked the entire night and most of the morning and they still hadn't found anything but trees. On the plus side, he'd had no more nightmares. He might yet come out of this with his sanity intact. On the negative side, they were running out of time.

Tarrys met his gaze, but didn't bother to answer. Not that he'd expected her to. He'd asked the same question every hour and she didn't know the answer any better now than she had the first dozen times. All they could do was keep walking and hope they stumbled upon the princess eventually. Really, how big could one forest be?

Damn big, apparently.

Tarrys's gaze turned front and he watched her, unable to take his focus off her for any amount of time. Even now, the birds followed them as if welcoming a conquering hero. He remembered the look in her eyes, the wonder that her race had once been more than slaves. That she was more. Watching her now as she strode through the forest with the grace and agility of a trained warrior, her head high, he had no trouble believing she was descended from a proud and ancient race. But he'd known she was more than a slave for a long time now. Since that day on the roof when he finally looked past her lack of hair and absence of human blood, looked into her and recognized the intelligence and strength within. She'd been a constant revelation to him, so the last few days were no surprise.

But whatever she was, she was Tarrys first and always. His partner. His…friend.

His.

He fought off the sudden attack of possessiveness. He had much bigger problems right now. Like finding and freeing Princess Ilaria before the gate opened, which he was beginning to think was akin to finding the holy grail. A myth and a damned impossible task.

He stifled a yawn, needing sleep, though not like before, when the poison had hit him with exhaustion he couldn't fight his way through. No, this was normal tiredness. He hadn't slept in more than a day and hadn't slept well in weeks.

Tarrys glanced at him with eyes that seemed to see right through him. "You need to rest."

"I'm good."

"Yes, but will you be tonight?"

"We'll rest before the attack. If there's time." They had to get through that gate tonight. There was no option. Now that the entire Esrian race knew a human was in this world, they'd be guarding the gates on this side just as the Sitheen had been guarding the gate on the Washington, D.C., side. If Harrison or any of the others tried to come after him, they'd be killed or captured before they ever got a chance to escape. No, he and Tarrys *had* to get through that gate tonight.

"I don't want to stop again until we find the temple village," he continued. "Or Ilaria. Is it possible we've hit more magic and are on some kind of treadmill, doomed to wander through here forever?"

He was half-joking, but the gaze she leveled on him held no humor. "I've been wondering if the temple village is shrouded so that we'll never see it."

Charlie groaned. "The forest likes you. It wouldn't do that to you, would it?"

"The forest might not. But the Esri control the village now."

"Would the Esri do that? Hide from us?"

"I doubt it. They'll want to kill you. They'll want to enslave me." She said the words so simply. As if she expected that outcome. Accepted it.

"How many Esri are with Ilaria? Do you know?"

"I know the story. Three hundred years ago, King Rith overthrew the queen and ordered her daughter, Princess Ilaria, confined to the forest. It's said there were three Esri immune to the forest's magic who delivered her here along with twenty Royal Guards to watch her and make certain she never left."

"Twenty to guard one woman in a place she couldn't possibly escape from?"

"Yes. After what I saw in that vision, I wonder if those three Esri were the same ones who overran the forest when the Marceils were here."

"Did those three return to court after the transfer?"

"No. The three were murdered as soon as the transfer was complete. Some suspect they were killed on the king's order so that the princess could never escape."

Two of them against twenty guards. If they were human guards, he wouldn't be that worried. He'd sneak up on them, one at a time, and take them out. But there would be no sneaking up, no quiet deaths, on this mission. Not only did the death chant result in a rather spectacular fireworks display, but with his death mark, every Esri knew where he was every minute of every day.

Disconcerting, to say the least.

Yet his only chance at reaching the princess was to take out her guards. All of them. Preferably from a distance.

"Have you ever shot a fire arrow?" he asked her.

"No." Her brow crinkled. "I would expect the fire to be extinguished by the wind of flight."

"It would be. Unless we wrap the points in cloth and find some kind of accelerant. Something to keep the cloth burning through the air."

"The sap of the thornewood tree burns."

"Perfect." They were everywhere. "How many arrows were you able to collect?"

"Six."

"We'll need more. At least twenty."

Tarrys nodded. "I'll make arrows while you sleep."

Charlie gave her shoulder a squeeze. "Let's find that village first."

"Hurry," the auburn-haired priestess urged her sisters. The three violet-eyed women pressed their hands to the trunk of a huge yellow tree. "The priestesses beg entrance to our chambers, oh tree of Esria." At once, a stair appeared, descending into the earth. The three women lifted gowns and ran lightly, if urgently, down the steps.

"Light," said the one whose love had just been captured. Torches flared, the light reflecting in the tears that streaked her face. "We must call the ancient power, or all is lost."

The small chamber, lit by two torches, was unfurnished except for a single wooden chest, but the walls were beautifully painted with scenes of musicians and dancers, of beautiful women and strong, handsome men. Lattice-work carved into the stone framed the scenes.

As one, the women ran to the chest and tore open the lid, each drawing out a brightly colored gossamer gown. Stripping off their plain shifts, they dressed hurriedly, then placed a pouch on a long cord around each of their necks, handed to them by the auburn-haired sister.

The third sister pulled an ornate vial from the chest and placed a drop of oil at the base of her throat and each of her sisters'.

"It is done," said the first. "Now we must reach the temple before the Esri do or all is lost."

The three ran up the stairs.

Tarrys slowly returned to herself, Charlie's face superimposed on the stairs until the latter disappeared and she saw only Charlie's worried expression.

He stood in front of her, his hands on her shoulders. "Are you okay?"

Tarrys nodded. "I saw a little more of what

happened in the past. The priestesses preparing for the ceremony they hoped would save their race."

His expression tightened with regret. Even without her seeing more, they both knew it hadn't worked. The Marceils had fallen.

"Do you remember the ruins we saw in the mist lands? I'm fairly sure they were Marceilian. Our civilization spread throughout these lands. I saw paintings, Charlie. We were once artists, musicians, dancers. And more, I think. Philosophers, mystics, seers. We were once the heart of this world. The soul. Without being told, I *know* that. Mine was once a proud and wise race."

Charlie squeezed her shoulders and pulled her against him. "I have no trouble believing that."

She wrapped her arms tight around him, pressed her cheek to his chest and clung to him against the buffeting sadness. "Once the gates to your world were closed and the Esri lost their human slaves, they turned on us. So much lost."

His hand stroked her hair and his gentleness and understanding brought tears to her eyes.

"At least you know," he murmured. "You may be the only Marceil in generations to know what your race once was."

Tarrys nodded, brushing her cheek against the silk of his tunic. "We were raised to believe the Marceils were never more than the slaves of the Esri."

It was too late for her race. More than a millennia too late. Even if the Esri went back to enslaving humans and chose to free the Marceils, their civilization was long gone. Lost and forgotten.

But it was not yet too late for the humans. Their fate would be the same as the Marceils', and on a far grander scale, if the Esri weren't stopped. A fury of determination swept through her as she tightened her hold on Charlie. If she had one purpose in her life, it was this. To save the human race from the same fate as her own.

So long as she remained free, the Esri would fail.

Chapter 23

"We're running out of time," Charlie growled. The sky had turned russet a couple of hours ago. The best he could figure, the gates would open in less than three hours, but he couldn't possibly know if his calculations were correct. This world was affected by the sun and moon of his own even if they didn't rise and set in the Esrian sky. Sunrise and sunset, or their equivalent, had shifted as they'd traveled, just as they would have in his world, moving from time zone to time zone, though far more quickly here. Both Tarrys and Kade had said they believed their world to be far smaller than his and he suspected they were right.

If he found the gate that was supposedly somewhere in this forest, he'd probably find himself in a completely different part of the world than D.C. But where, he couldn't begin to guess. And unless they found their way through these endless woods, nothing else was going to matter. Not arrows, which they didn't have enough of. Not gates, which neither of them had the ability to locate. Not even the Esri.

Tarrys stopped suddenly, her wide-eyed gaze whirling toward him.

"What's the matter?"

"I hear something. Music."

Charlie listened. He was about to shake his head when he heard it. The faint strains from some kind of medieval-sounding stringed instrument drifted to him on the ever-present breeze. "The Esri like music? I thought torture was more their speed."

"All people enjoy music."

Charlie gripped her shoulder, relief and adrenaline flooding his system. "We're almost there."

Tarrys pointed left. "Look. I see the faint glow of a red crystal. Do you see it?"

Charlie dug his binoculars out of his gear vest, put them to his eyes and followed the direction she pointed. Sure enough, he could definitely make out the red glow and part of a structure of some kind. No people, but he was looking at a very tiny slice from a large distance.

He lowered his binoculars. "That has to be the clearing. If we'd continued the way we were going, we'd have walked right by it."

"Which is probably why they played the music. To catch our attention."

Charlie looked at her, the comment making him pause. "Damn. I keep thinking we're sneaking up on them, but they know right where we are, don't they? They've been following our progress, waiting for us to come to them."

"Waiting for *you* to come to them. It's your death mark they follow. They might not even know I'm here."

He looked at her sharply, not liking the sound of that. "You're not going in there alone."

"I won't leave the forest. I just want to take a look around and see where they're holding Princess Ilaria."

The rust of the night sky did little to light the forest, casting her face in shadow. But he recognized the determined jut of her chin.

"All right. But I'll be right behind you."

Her head tilted. "That defeats the purpose, doesn't it?"

"Doesn't matter." His need to protect her grew stronger every day, every hour. It was all he could do not to order her to remain deep in the forest and let him handle the Esri alone. But he needed her help. "I'm not going to let them have you. We believe none of them can enter the forest, but what if we're wrong?"

"Charlie, with your death mark, they know where you are every second. If you go anywhere near that clearing, they'll attack you. Either let me scout out the situation alone, or we go together and take out as many Esri as we can with the arrows we have."

She was right, dammit.

"Wait. I brought something that might be helpful." He dug under his tunic, grabbed a lighter and slipped a folded piece of paper out of one of his pockets. He turned his back on the forest, flicked the lighter and illuminated the page. "Just a reminder who we're looking for."

Tarrys moved beside him to look at the photograph of a painting of an Esrian woman standing in a human forest. When the Sitheen were researching the whereabouts of the seven stones, they'd stumbled upon this and another painting that Kade had eventually confirmed depicted Princess Ilaria. Apparently the nineteenth-century Danish painter had been a Sitheen who'd seen Princess Ilaria…and Esria…in his visions.

"If the stories are true, she's the only woman here."

Charlie grunted. "The last thing we need is to get home only to find we rescued the wrong woman." He snuffed the light, pocketed the folded paper and reached for her, cupping her shadowed face in his hands. "Stay deep in the trees and don't take any risks. Promise?"

"I promise."

She met his kiss, hers as fiercely delivered as his own then he pulled back, forcing his hands to release her.

"Be careful."

"Always." He caught the flash of a smile before she turned and took off running with her usual lithe grace, her steps sure and silent.

His heart pounded with fear for her as it never did for himself. How would he survive if he lost her?

Tarrys ran through the dark woods, marveling anew that in this lonely forest, her people had once thrived. In this place of fears, she belonged.

Above her, the soft whoosh of bird wings sounded overhead, the birds following her still, though the other creatures had disappeared as night fell.

When she'd traveled far enough that the Esri shouldn't be watching this direction, she turned back toward the clearing and stopped as something in the forest caught her eye—a tree in the distance, its yellow bark glowing faintly.

Her pulse began to race as she stared at it, recognizing the tree from the second vision. The tree that had marked the priestesses' secret chamber.

Chill bumps rose on her arms. Could the chamber still be there even though the priestesses were long gone? Likely no one had been in that place since that fateful day. No one had gazed on those paintings, nor ever would again.

She thought of the sisters, and of the lovers torn apart before they'd ever truly been together. The look she'd seen in the man's eyes made her own burn with unwanted tears. So much love destroyed. She wanted to believe the two had found a way, somehow, to be together. But she knew the Esri. She knew what life was like for the enslaved.

As she started toward the clearing, her heart felt heavy with sadness. How much harder must it have been for those who'd known freedom and power? For those learned, talented men and women with rich lives and deep loves to have their lives stripped from them? To have their loves sold off or raped before their eyes?

No, it was better to never have known such freedom. Even for her now, going back to enslavement would be a thousand times worse than it had been before.

Silently, she crept toward the clearing until the red glow separated, revealing red, blue and orange crystals scattered among the structures. Even the structures themselves began to take shape through the veil of trees. The village clearing appeared wide, easily as large as a human's city block, dotted with roofless structures that appeared to have been hewn from the wood of the forest trees, then sanded, carved and painted with intricate care. They appeared to be furnished in the Esrian fashion with tables and stools, the columns draped with long lengths of colorful silks, the benches and floors littered with pillows in every hue.

In the center of the clearing stood the temple the priestesses had spoken of, rising high above the other structures, strong and proud. Built of red stone, the temple stood as high as a three-story apartment building, built in the shape of a pyramid, its four sides made of stairs rising to the very top. Each stair appeared to have been painted with small, intricate designs. Swirls, perhaps? Or flowers?

She could almost imagine what it would have been like all those years ago, the ancient Marceils walking through the temple village with pride, discussing and debating issues of the mind as a child laughed and scampered around them. Musicians playing, dancers moving in graceful dances between the pillars. And lovers walking hand in hand, dreams in their eyes.

Now the village served as a prison, though the only structure that might possibly hold anyone was the temple itself. Was the princess being held there? Was there any need to hold her at all, given that she couldn't escape the clearing?

Tarrys crept closer and closer until she finally had an unobstructed view. Of the Esri.

Her pulse leaped to her throat as she saw them, their backs pressed to the trees Charlie would pass if he attempted to breach the village. Each Esri held either a bow or a knife glittering in the crystal light. She could shoot them so easily from here, but without the fire from Charlie's lighter, and his whispering the death chant, her arrows would do nothing but cause them a few seconds of pain.

A movement along the side of the structure closest to Charlie drew her attention. *A woman.* She was tied to one of the columns, standing tall and proud, her pale hair threaded with ribbons and plaited down her back, her royal emerald gown in perfect repair. As she lifted her face into the light of the nearest crystal, Tarrys got a clear look at her. Princess Ilaria.

And she was no prisoner. Not dressed and groomed to such perfection. Not when she stood conveniently tied at the edge of the clearing, the very edge the Esri expected Charlie to walk through.

Clearly, the Esri had no respect for the intelligence of humans or they'd never have set such an obvious trap.

She counted sixteen Esri guards, when she'd expected twenty. That was good. With enough arrows, she could pick off the sixteen, freeing Charlie to rescue…or capture…Princess Ilaria.

Hope lifted on a rush of excitement. They were going to succeed. In the next few hours, she'd make the arrows she needed. Then with her fire arrows and Charlie's death chant, they'd destroy the Esri guards and steal Ilaria.

They were going to make it.

But as she turned to retrace her steps, a flash of white detached itself from the shadows and lunged for her.

An Esri.

Tarrys dove right to avoid his reaching hands, but he caught her quiver, tearing it from her back. His other hand caught her hair.

Fury roared through her, a fury as much for her race as for herself, for destruction and degradation and cruelty beyond conscience. Ripping the bow from her shoulder she shoved it up and back, hard into the Esri's face. Her attacker roared with pain, releasing her hair. But when she leaped free, he snatched the bow from her hands.

For an instant, she faced him, debating trying to retrieve her precious bow. But he lunged at her and she spun and ran.

The Esri's footsteps followed behind her, pounding at half the speed of her heart, until ending abruptly on a shout of fear. She didn't look back, knowing the forest had risen to her defense, attacking him with a nightmare. Not until she saw Charlie racing toward her did she slow to a walk.

Tears burned her eyes. She'd lost her arrows, her quiver, her bow.

Charlie swept her into his arm, pulling her against him as her arms went around his neck.

"He hurt you."

"No." She was shaking with the aftershock of fear. Desolate with loss. "I didn't see him."

His arms tightened around her. "It wasn't your fault."

"He took my bow. My arrows." A sob caught in her throat. "Charlie, I lost everything. Our only chance."

"Shh." He let her slide to her feet, but still held her against him. "We'll manage. We'll make more arrows. Another bow."

She pulled back, meeting his gaze. "There isn't time. And there's more you must know. They've tied Princess Ilaria to a column, but she's not a prisoner."

"How do you know?"

"Her hair and her gown have been beautifully tended, as have the clearing structures. Her guards serve her, I'm sure of it."

"It makes sense. They've been trapped here together for centuries."

"Tying her was a ploy to draw you in."

"She doesn't know I'm here to rescue her. Did you see the guards?"

"Yes. They're hiding behind the trees, ready to attack you when you come for her."

"Twenty?"

"I saw sixteen. Plus the one who came after me. The others could have been anywhere. If I'd had the fire arrows…"

The vision came on her suddenly. She shot out a hand as if to stop it, but it yanked her into a free fall across fifteen centuries. And when she emerged again, she knew why the forest had shown her these visions.

She knew what she had to do. And where to find the courage.

In Charlie's arms.

Chapter 24

Charlie held Tarrys against his heart until the vision passed, hating the tears streaming down her cheeks. He was sitting on the ground, Tarrys on his lap beneath a thick-trunked tree.

"Don't cry, sweetheart." He stroked her soft hair. "It's okay."

Slowly, she came out of it only to fling her arms around his neck and bury her face against his throat, sobbing as if her heart were breaking.

"Tarrys. Don't cry."

Finally, when her tears were spent, she pulled back and slid her palms over his cheeks. Her gaze fell to his mouth and she leaned forward and touched her salty lips to his.

He kissed her back with infinite gentleness, letting her lead, waiting for her to tell him what she'd seen even as he knew all too well—the Marceils captured, raped, enslaved.

"Make love with me, Charlie," she whispered against his mouth. "Please make love with me."

She looked up at him, her eyes filled with wrenching sadness and a desperate longing. And almost unbearable grief. She thought he was going to die, he realized. And maybe he was.

Her breath brushed warm across his mouth. "Make love with me."

Need rose inside him, swift and fierce, his hands tightening at her waist.

"Tarrys…" A hundred reasons why this was neither the time nor the place flew through his mind. He should be out there trying to kill as many Esri as he could. But how, when they knew where he was at every moment and were waiting to kill him?

The word *hopeless* rang through his head. There was virtually nothing he could do in the short time left to improve his nearly nonexistent chances of success.

Tarrys kissed him, her soft, desperate heat spearing through him.

There was nothing he could do but this. Loving this woman. Living while life was still his.

Charlie kissed her back, the desire he'd worked so hard to ignore rushing in, unleashed. In this moment, she was his to kiss, his to love. And nothing mattered but this moment. And Tarrys.

His arms went around her as he pulled her tight against his chest, kissing her, inhaling her. Affection welled inside him, until he thought he couldn't contain it all. She was courage and sweetness, strength and light. His beginning and ultimately, too soon, his end.

Her hands slid into his hair and she kissed him as fiercely as he kissed her, her tongue sweeping inside his mouth, sliding over his.

Tarrys. Her name echoed through his head and poured into his heart, lighting him from inside with a flame that was as much warmth as heat, as much tenderness as desire.

Her hips rocked against his, brushing his erection, telling him in no uncertain terms what she wanted. What they both wanted. He reached down, grabbed twin fistfuls of her gown and yanked it out from under her rear until he could reach beneath. His fingers sank into the soft warmth of her buttocks, drawing a low moan from her throat as he kissed her, before sliding down the firm, slender thighs spread across his lap. He longed to touch her everywhere, to touch her until she screamed for release. There wasn't time for such luxury. Later, when they got home...

A stab of harsh regret buried itself in his chest and he kissed Tarrys harder, shoving back the future and turning the whole of his attention to the woman in his arms, the woman whose thighs were so sweetly parted for him. As her hips rocked against him, his fingers slid to her buttocks, then down to the moist center of her heat.

Her gasp pulled the breath from his mouth as she melted against him. So sweet. He slid his finger inside her and she turned frantic, her fingers digging into his scalp, her mouth crazy with need, her body rocking against him until he thought he'd explode.

He had to touch her. With shaking hands, he yanked her gown up and over her head until she was naked before him. As his hands covered her breasts, their hard tips tight against his palms, she met his gaze with eyes glazed with passion. She leaned forward to kiss his jaw, her lips moving down his neck, sending fire flaming through his blood.

"I want you inside me," she said against his throat. "Love me, Charlie. Love me."

His thoughts fled, his senses hijacked. Tarrys. She was all he could ever want. All he could ever need. He wasn't even aware he'd undressed until he was moving over her, flesh against flesh, her breasts brushing against his chest.

Her hands slid over his shoulders as if the feel of him pleased her. "Love me, Charlie Rand. Make love to me."

Looking down into her shadowed face, he pushed inside her with a single stroke, the intensity of his own pleasure mirrored in her face. Emotion swelled until it pressed against the walls of his chest. He pulled out of her and slid home a second time, and a third. Over and over, harder and harder, she rose to meet him, joining with him until he no longer knew where he ended and she began.

Deep in his consciousness, the storm began to rise, buffeting him, threatening to sweep him overboard and drown him if he didn't hold firm, if he didn't protect his heart.

The fury of their lovemaking grew as Tarrys's moans rose and his own body climbed higher with every thrust.

Let go, Charlie. Come with me. Tarrys's voice. In his head. In his heart. *Fly with me.*

The pressure in his chest wouldn't be contained. His control was lost. His heart was hers.

Charlie covered her mouth, clinging to her as he thrust into her, as he let go. The storm of emotions rushed through him, sweeping him up, higher and higher.

Fly with me.

She cried out her release, her soft contractions lifting him to his own. As the release broke over him, he let go. And flew on wings born of the overpowering love for her he'd been fighting, denying. And could deny no more.

He loved her. Loved Tarrys.

The thought terrified even as it liberated. He loved her and would continue to love her with every breath he took until he breathed no more.

He kissed her, kept kissing her even as he pulled out of her and rolled onto his back, pulling her across him so he could kiss her some more.

"I love you." He'd said the words out loud.

Words he'd never told any woman. Words he'd never thought he could say.

He felt like a man reborn. The irony nearly made him laugh. Reborn. As he stared down death.

Tarrys pulled away from his kisses and looked at him, propping her arms on his chest. He expected to see happiness in her eyes. He loved her! But her eyes were drenched with sadness.

He lifted a hand to cup her cheek. "Tarrys…"

She pressed her fingers to his lips. "Charlie, I have to go."

He stared at her, not understanding. "Go where?"

"I have to leave. I'm so sorry. But I've seen things in my visions. I have responsibilities to my people I didn't know I had. My place is here. I'm not going back with you."

He blinked and sat up as she scooted off him. "You think I'm going to die. You're leaving now so you don't have to watch." He couldn't believe it. Her lack of faith…

She touched his cheek. "You're not going to die. If you wait for the gates to open, you'll succeed."

"How can you possibly know that?"

Her expression was at once powerfully sure and infinitely sad. "I know, Charlie. You'll take Princess Ilaria back and save your world. But I can't go with you. I'm needed here." She rose, slipping on her slave's gown with a single, graceful movement.

He stared at her, as stunned by her words that he was going to succeed as he was by the fact she was leaving anyway. Leaving him. After he'd told her he loved her.

As she stood before him, her eyes bright with unshed tears, he wanted to rise, but couldn't move for the weight crushing his chest.

"Wait until the gates open before you free her, Charlie."

"How in the hell am I supposed to know when the gates open?"

"Look to the sky." A single tear slid down her cheek. "I love you, Charlie Rand." Another tear followed, and another. "Don't forget me." She turned and ran, lithe as a deer, leaving him stunned and reeling, struggling for air.

An awful sense of déjà vu washed over him. Ten years old, his dad standing before him. "I have to leave, son. I can't be with you boys and your mother anymore. I love you, Charlie. But I can't stay." Charlie had never seen him again. He'd never even heard from him.

Dammit. He leaped to his feet and slammed the heel of his hand against the nearest tree as fury sliced through him. "Damn her to *hell*."

Why had he told her he loved her? Why had he *let* himself love her? He wasn't meant for love. He'd never been meant for love.

If she'd loved him, really loved him, why had she left?

He pulled on his clothes with angry yanks. He didn't need her. Love never lasted anyway. Within a couple of days, he'd forget about her.

Damn her for following him here in the first place. If she'd just stayed back in D.C. like he told her to...

He took a big breath and let it out slowly.

He'd be dead.

If she'd stayed in D.C. like he'd told her to, he'd never have discovered her strength or her courage. He'd never have tasted the sweetness of her kiss or the shattering ecstasy of making love with the woman who'd been made for him. His match. His mate.

Pain clenched its fist around his heart. He sank to the ground, leaning back against a tree. How was he supposed to live without her? She was his life, his breath.

His heart.

He wasn't sure how long he'd sat there waiting for God knew what. A half hour? Longer?

Something glittered in his vision and he blinked, but it didn't go away. He looked up… and stilled.

Stars. The russet Esrian sky glittered with a million of them.

The gate was open.

Chills raced over his skin. The worlds were

one, and yet…not. He couldn't wrap his mind around it, but he didn't have to. Not now.

What he had to do now was free Princess Ilaria without getting himself killed, and convince her to show him to the nearest gate. And do it within the hour or that gate was going to close and he'd be stuck here for another month.

Harrison and Jack would try to follow him in and almost certainly die. But the thought of going through that gate alone, of leaving Tarrys behind, tore a fresh wound in his heart.

Focus. Compartmentalize. Because if he kept thinking about Tarrys, he'd never succeed.

Charlie rose and pressed his hands against the tree, head bent, taking deep breaths. He was a soldier. A SEAL. *Focus.* Right now he had to concentrate on beating these bastards and freeing the potentially duplicitous Ilaria. Right now he had to keep himself alive and save the world.

He took a mental inventory of his gear, then shook his head. There was no possible way he was going to succeed without a miracle. Then again, this land was magic. And this forest hated the Esri.

He pulled out one of his small flamethrowers and his knife. One in each hand, he ran silently through the woods, toward the clearing. If he were stalking humans, they'd never know he was coming.

As he drew near, an arrow whizzed by his shoulder.

Unfortunately, this enemy was not human.

He rolled behind a tree as two more arrows broke the air he'd been occupying a second before. Any thought that the Esri might want to capture him was gone. They clearly wanted him dead.

Adrenaline poured through his system, raising his spirits. God, he loved a challenge.

Two more arrows passed on either side of the tree, pinning him in place. He was still nearly twenty yards from the temple. Could the Esri come this far into the forest? Would they risk it in order to capture him?

He was all too afraid the answer was yes. His

gaze landed on one of the arrows sticking out of a tree in front of him. If only Tarrys were here with her bow to give him a moment's cover. But he was on his own now.

Shoving his knife in his boot, he pulled out his binoculars and tried to get a bead on his attackers. Two archers stood in plain sight, aiming for him. A short distance behind them, he could make out the form of a woman tied to a pillar of stone. *Ilaria.* She was every bit as beautiful as the painting he'd seen of her, and yet her beauty didn't hold a candle to Tarrys's.

The archers released their arrows and he ducked back as the projectiles flew by him. The Esri had apparently abandoned their plan to trap him. Then again, they knew Tarrys had seen the setup. They knew it wouldn't work.

Yet Ilaria remained tied. Why? To confuse him? Or because they feared she'd try to escape? Even well-treated prisoners longed for freedom.

Another arrow sailed past him.

"I could use your help, forest," he muttered. "Can you extend your influence into the clearing? Scare the crap out of them for me, maybe?"

He didn't expect an answer, but the sudden gust of wind that whipped at his cloak, sent chills racing over his flesh. The wind rose, tossing leaves and swirling his cloak around his body.

There was no weather in Esria.

Yeah, things were definitely getting interesting, though how a storm was going to help him, he couldn't begin to guess. Maybe it would confuse the Esri? He couldn't afford to be picky. He needed any help he could get.

Charlie dove out from behind the tree and rolled behind another, but no arrows followed him. He dove and rolled again and still no arrows.

Cautiously, he eased out, close enough to see the Esri now that he knew where to look. They were still aiming where he'd been two trees ago. As if they hadn't seen him move.

He frowned.

With extreme caution, he ran forward, from tree to tree, keeping watch on the two archers as he scanned for others. As he neared the clearing, more Esri came into view, all clustered around Ilaria and the other archers. To a man, unmoving.

Frozen.

His eyes widened as his gaze snagged on one Esri caught in midstride, his cloak whipping around him in the punishing wind, one foot lifted, extended, paralyzed several inches off the ground.

No. Way.

This was it, then. His chance. He'd needed a miracle and the forest had delivered it on a platter.

"Thanks, woods," he said.

Still scanning for sign of danger, he ran for Ilaria, fully aware he might not have much time. His senses cataloged a large, ruined village surrounding an Aztec-style pyramid. But Ilaria was thankfully close to the edge of the forest, if a tad too close to the Esri. If that wind died too soon, he was dead.

Princess Ilaria—and he knew it was her, for she was the spitting image of the woman in the painting—stood as frozen as her guards, her emerald gown twisting around her legs. Her hair, pale ivory streaked with gold, flew around her porcelain-like face. Eyes as green as her gown followed him, sharp and cunning. He might be performing a rescue, but he'd be smart to treat her with the care and caution he would any dangerous animal.

"I've come to rescue you, Princess," he shouted against the wind. Maybe that would keep her from attacking him if she got the chance, though with an Esri, he couldn't be too careful. Just because she'd sealed the gates fifteen centuries ago didn't mean she considered herself a friend to humans. She might not have done it to help the humans. And she might not be willing to do it again. But she was their only chance of getting those gates sealed. They'd do what they must to force her to help them. But first he had to get her out of this forest, out of Esria.

He cut through the ropes binding her, then retied her hands behind her back, slung her over his shoulder and ran for the woods away from the archers. When they came back to life, they wouldn't have him in their sights.

The problem was, he still didn't know where the gate was. He needed the princess to tell him. If she wasn't able to talk before the gate closed again, this rescue was going to be for nothing.

The wind blew fiercely as he ran across the golden grasses of the clearing, the princess slung over his back. He was nearly to the woods on the other side when lightning flashed across the sky, half-blinding him as it arced toward the center of the village. The pyramid must be acting like some kind of lightning rod. Another flash tore across the sky. His gaze followed it to the structure…and froze.

At the top of the pyramid, on what appeared to be a small platform, stood a jewel of a woman in a sheer-as-mist lavender gown. Her long brown hair flew in the wind, her arms raised as if she called the lightning, called down the very storm.

Tarrys. His heart seized as her tear-filled gaze found him, clinging to him for one wrenching moment before turning skyward again, piercing his heart.

Chapter 25

The ancient power ripped through Tarrys, crushing her beneath its weight, but she held fast even as every bone in her body felt like it was about to crumble.

"Run, Charlie! Run." Her words weren't enough to reach her own ears, let alone his, but he'd stopped just inside the tree line when he'd seen her. He had to move. He had to go or all this was for nothing. "Run!"

Tarrys gasped at the pain wrought by the power. She hadn't expected the pain, hadn't realized her ancestress was in pain when she'd watched her in that final vision, the one that had come upon her soon after she'd lost her bow and quiver. But seeing that last vision, she'd finally understood. After leaving Charlie, she'd gone to the yellow tree, called for it to open and found the chamber just as the three priestesses had left it. Even their discarded shifts lay on the floor exactly where she'd watched them drop them all those centuries ago. She'd chosen a fine gown as they had, put a pouch around her neck as they had theirs. As she'd felt the fine silk of the ceremonial gown slide around her body, soft and damning, she'd known her fate was destined to be the same as theirs. The memory of that vision wouldn't leave her.

The three sisters ran for the temple. They weren't sisters in blood or parentage, but in the power passed to them from the ancient priestesses, power marked by the color of their eyes. Only the violet-eyes could call the power of the ancients. Only the priestesses could save their race now. The eldest of the three led the way, tears on her cheeks as she cried for the lover torn from her, for the mating ceremony that would never come.

The temple village was in chaos. Marceils, their scalps hacked and bleeding, attacked their brothers, wives, even children, cutting off their hair and pinning them down until one of the Esri came to lay a hand on them, claiming their will. The sisters ran through the hair and blood, dodging the reaching hands even as they met the pleading gazes with the promise of deliverance.

The first of the sisters never made it to the temple stairs before she was caught and dragged beneath the enslaver's knife. The auburn-haired priestess made it nearly to the top, but was felled by an Esri's arrow only to tumble down the long stairs and fall beneath a different blade.

The eldest and last of the priestesses reached the sacred altar at the very top and raised her hands to the sky, calling on the ancient powers. Wind tore at her hair and lightning rode her fingers as she stole the Esri's control, immobilizing them where they stood.

She cried for the Marceils to take them down and bind them. But none answered. There were no Marceils left free to act. All but her had already been enslaved.

"All is lost," she cried. And then she saw him, her love, his thick hair reduced to random clumps, his scalp covered in dried blood. He began to climb the temple stairs.

His eyes glistened with sorrow and grief and spilled bitter tears as he reached her and drew his knife.

"No," she whispered. "Don't do this."

"If I could turn this blade on myself, I would. But he controls my every move. Forgive me, my love."

Tarrys's gaze turned outward again and she met Charlie's across the storm-tossed village. The power was becoming too much for her to hold, but it didn't matter. He was nearly to the forest, nearly safe. *Run, Charlie!* The power escaped her grasp and she collapsed to her knees, too weak to run. But she'd known there would be no escape. She'd done what she'd needed to do. She'd given Charlie a chance to free the princess and escape the village. Now he needed the princess free to act again, free to lead him to the gate, and safety.

The rest was up to Charlie, now. She'd done all she could.

As one, the Esri sprang to life, running for the temple in a race to reach her first, to claim her as a slave. The pounding of their climbing steps came at her from every direction.

"Run, Charlie," she whispered. Tarrys held his gaze as rough hands grabbed her from behind, as the searing pain of a sharp knife tore at the flesh of her skull over and over and over. She held his gaze until blood ran into her eyes, mixing with her tears, and all she could see was a future as bleak and cold as her past.

But Charlie had a chance.

It was enough.

Charlie watched the Esri attack Tarrys, feeling every stroke of the knife as if it sliced through his own heart. His eyes burned as understanding crashed over him, slamming him back. She hadn't left him.

She'd sacrificed herself to save him.

"Release the Marceil," he yelled. "And I'll give you back your princess!"

"No. Leave her," his captive said imperiously. "The gate will not remain open long. You need me to find it. I need you to get me through the forest."

Charlie swung her off his shoulder and onto her feet, gripping her upper arm. "I'm not leaving without her."

Bright eyes peered at him curiously. "She's just a slave."

"She's the woman I love."

Princess Ilaria made a sound of pure frustration. But she turned and shouted, "Sanderis, release your Marceil."

"Nay, Princess. She's mine."

"He knows the death chant, Sanderis. King Rith may be glad to see me dead…or he may have other plans for me. Are you willing to risk his anger?"

Charlie heard the arrow a second before it buried itself in the tree six inches to his right.

"Charlie, leave!" Tarrys's cry turned into a scream of pain, but he could no longer see her.

"Make them free her!" Charlie growled at his captive.

To his surprise, the princess began to tremble beneath his grip, her gaze beginning to flick left and right with fear. The forest, he realized, was already starting on her.

"Sanderis!" The princess's voice held a note of terror the Esri finally responded to. The moment he released Tarrys, she flew down the temple steps and through the clearing, tears and blood streaking her face.

His heart broke. As she neared, he let go of the princess to sweep Tarrys into his arms and hold her tight against him.

"Free the princess, human!" the Esri shouted. Another arrow flew by, just missing him.

"We've got to get out of here." He released Tarrys and turned to the other woman. "Princess Ilaria, where's the gate?"

But the woman didn't answer, her eyes wide with fear, her body quaking. Tarrys grabbed the woman's pale arm. "Don't see it, Princess. It's not there."

Ilaria blinked and drew in a shuddering breath, but seemed far from relieved. She was still shaking badly.

"The gate, Ilaria?" Charlie prompted. "We're out of time."

Slowly her gaze focused on him and her head began to nod. "That way. Nearly a quarter of a mile. We must hurry."

With one hand, Charlie grabbed Ilaria's bound arm, holding her up as she ran. His other was tight around Tarrys and he had no intention of ever letting her go.

They flew through the woods as quickly as possible, but Charlie kept glancing at the stars overhead. Unless his eyes were playing tricks on him, they were fading fast.

"There," Ilaria said.

"I see it," Tarrys said. "It's closing!"

Charlie released Ilaria, watching as she disappeared into thin air. A moment later, Charlie jerked Tarrys hard against him and followed, diving once more into chaos.

The cold wind bit and stung, yet Tarrys had never felt warmer as she sat beneath the human's full moon and stroked the head she cradled in her lap. The head of the man she loved beyond life, beyond reason.

Charlie Rand.

As before, the trip through the gate had temporarily knocked him out.

Charlie blinked with confusion, the whites of his eyes reflecting the moon's glow, then sat up and leaped to his feet in a single move, his gaze swinging from her to Ilaria and back again, assessing the situation, searching for danger.

"Have you seen anyone? Heard anything?" he asked, his voice low.

"No," Tarrys replied. "It's quiet here. And cold."

"It's too dark to be anywhere on the East Coast of the U.S. Has Ilaria touched you?"

"No."

"I have no need for your slave, human," Ilaria said, sitting a few feet away, her hands still tied behind her back, the moonlight turning her hair silver.

Slowly, Charlie sank to his knees beside Tarrys and pulled her into his arms, his strong arms wrapping tight around her as he kissed her with an urgency and fierceness that brought tears to her eyes.

She kissed him back, tears slipping down her cheeks as she clung to him, her heart still pounding in her chest. She'd risked everything for him, everything. And he'd nearly thrown it away.

Wrenching back, she chided him. "You should have run when you had the chance. They could have killed you. You risked your life…your world…to save me."

She felt his hands slide gently along her ruined scalp in the dark. Though the flesh had healed, only tufts of her hair remained. "I would have sacrificed a thousand worlds for you. I love you." Though she wished she could see his eyes, he kissed her, telling her through the gentle urgency of his mouth and hands, the truth of his words.

"Marry me, Tarrys," he said against her mouth.

Tarrys pulled back, afraid to believe. "Charlie, you can't really..."

"I do."

"But I'm not human, I'm..."

His lips brushed over hers in a tender caress. "I know what you are. Better than you do, I think. Brave, strong, wise and beautiful, you're my life. My heart." He kissed her again, whispering into the dark. "I didn't understand love before I met you. You showed me that miracle. You're my destiny, Tarrys. The one I've been waiting for. Without you, my life means nothing."

His hands slid along her jaw, his thumbs stroking her cheeks. "I want you beside me every day for the rest of my life, sweetheart, but I won't push you. I don't want you to feel like you have to do anything you don't want to do ever again."

Tarrys stared into his moon-drenched eyes. "I've loved you since the moment I met you, Charlie. I never dared dream you could love me back."

"I do. Now, will you please tell me you'll marry me so I can call Harrison to come get us out of here?"

Tarrys laughed, her heart lighter than she'd ever imagined. Her joy complete. "Yes. A thousand times yes."

* * * * *

Mills & Boon® Online

Discover more romance at
www.millsandboon.co.uk

- **FREE** online reads
- **Books** up to one month before shops
- **Browse our books** before you buy

...and much more!

For exclusive competitions and instant updates:

 Like us on **facebook.com/romancehq**

 Follow us on **twitter.com/millsandboonuk**

 Join us on **community.millsandboon.co.uk**

Visit us Online Sign up for our FREE eNewsletter at
www.millsandboon.co.uk

WEB/M&B/RTL4/LP